THE LEGO MOVIE

JUNIOR NOVEL

THE LEGO MOVIE

JUNIOR NOVEL

Adapted by Kate Howard
from the screenplay by
PHIL LORD & CHRISTOPHER MILLER
Story by DAN HAGEMAN & KEVIN HAGEMAN
and PHIL LORD & CHRISTOPHER MILLER

Scholastic Inc.

Special thanks to
Matthew James Ashton and Katrine Talks

ISBN 978-0-545-62464-0

12 11 10 9 8 7 6 5 4 3 2 1 14 15 16 17 18 19/0

Printed in the U.S.A. 40

First printing, January 2014

CONTENTS

A SPECIAL ANNOUNCEMENT FROM THE MASTER BUILDER VITRUVIUS

The world was once free and full of possibility. Then came order, and after it, authority. Everything changed . . . until nothing changed at all.

Now evil seeks an ultimate power — a weapon called the Kragle that is a means to absolute control. But there is yet hope: a Piece of Resistance.

There is also an important prophecy that will guide the good guys in their quest to find the Piece of Resistance and defeat Lord Business and his evil ways. This true and important and very real (really *real*!) prophecy states:

> *One day a talented lass or fellow . . .*
> *A Special One with face of yellow . . .*
> *Will make the Piece of Resistance found . . .*
> *From its hiding refuge underground.*

And with a noble army at the helm . . .
This Master Builder will thwart the Kragle and save the realm . . .
And be the greatest, most interesting, most important person of all times . . .
All this is true because it rhymes.

Some may not believe the prophecy, but others will. Those smarty-pants believe it holds the power to save the universe from the Kragle and Lord Business and his plans for world domination.

Consider this a warning from me, Vitruvius, a trustworthy wizard dude with a beard. Follow the Prophecy of the Kragle, and protect the Piece of Resistance. The fate of the universe is in the hands of the special person who finds it. He or she will lead us to victory.

(Also, in case you have any doubts, remember: You should always trust any wizard guys who have important-looking beards. It's just the smart thing to do.)

1

Bright red lava flowed from the volcano that marked the entrance to the hidden temple. Inside, a mighty weapon called the Kragle was nestled in a glowing sarcophagus. The wizard Vitruvius stood at the temple's entrance, guarding the Kragle from the evil that approached.

"He is coming," Vitruvius said, turning to the guards on either side of him. "Cover your tush."

"Cover what?" One of the guards looked around, confused.

An instant later, the temple door burst open,

knocking the guards into a steaming pool of lava. A tall, dark figure in a cape and helmet swept into the temple with an army of robots at his side.

"Vitruvius," declared the menacing figure, sizing up the wizard.

"Lord Business." Vitruvius stared back. He was unimpressed.

Lord Business nodded. "You've hidden the Kragle well, old man." He flashed his cape. "Now step aside and let Mr. Big Boy Pants have it. I promise I will do you no harm."

Vitruvius stood his ground. "The only harm I fear is the harm you will do to the entire world if the Kragle falls into your hands."

"Your wordplay is weak," Lord Business chuckled. He didn't exactly understand everything Vitruvius said. Sometimes, he suspected the old wizard liked confusing people with his weird speeches. "Robots, destroy him!"

"Yes, Lord Business," the robots answered in a monotone.

Vitruvius was not afraid. His creations could get him out of any bind. After all, he was a Master Builder, one of the greatest and most important people in the history of the universe.

"Your robots are no match for a Master Builder, for I see everything," he told Lord Business.

Vitruvius glanced around the temple, taking

stock of the LEGO pieces that surrounded him. Suddenly, he began to construct the perfect defense: a flock of superstrong eagles that could conquer even the evilest of evil lords.

But before he could finish, the robots aimed a laser pointer right at Vitruvius's eyes, blinding him. "My eyes! *Ow!*" Vitruvius screeched, falling to his knees.

Lord Business smirked at the wizard's misfortune. With Vitruvius out of the way, there was nothing standing between him and the Kragle. He swept over to the sarcophagus and threw it open.

A brilliant glow burst forth, illuminating Lord Business's dark silhouette. "UH-HUH! OH, YEAH!" He fist-pumped. "The Kragle—the most powerful super weapon—is mine!"

Lord Business felt overwhelmed with power at simply being near such a great and magical piece. "Now my evil power will be unlimited. Can you feel me?"

"I can feel you," one of his robots replied.

"Woo!" Lord Business cheered as his robots picked up the sarcophagus. "Nothing's gonna stop me now!"

The moment the sarcophagus was removed from its resting place, the volcano rumbled, and the temple walls began to collapse. Lord Business

and his robots hastily headed for the exit.

"Wait . . ." Vitruvius moaned. "There is a prophecy."

Lord Business stopped, turned, and rolled his eyes. "Oh, now there's a prophecy?"

"About the Piece of Resistance . . ." Vitruvius continued.

"Oh, yes," Lord Business sneered. "The supposed missing Piece of Resistance that can somehow magically disarm the Kragle. Give me a break." *Wizards always come up with the most ridiculous stuff,* he thought.

Vitruvius looked slightly possessed as he pronounced:

One day a talented lass or fellow . . .
A Special One with face of yellow . . .
Will make the Piece of Resistance found . . .
From its hiding refuge underground.

And with a noble army at the helm . . .
This Master Builder will thwart the Kragle and save the realm . . .
And be the greatest, most interesting, most important person of all times . . .
All this is true because it rhymes.

"Oh, that was a great, inspiring legend," Lord

Business said sarcastically. "You made it up, didn't you?" He kicked Vitruvius into a pit. Then he turned and led his robot army out of the crumbling temple. "'A Special One'? I mean, come *on*. What a bunch of hippie-dippie baloney."

2

The sound of a clock radio blaring woke Emmet. He smiled and leaped out of bed. He was ready to greet the day with the kind of regular-guy fun that made his life so perfectly normal. "Good morning, apartment! Good morning, doorway. Morning, wall."

Emmet headed to his bookshelf. "Good morning, ceiling. Good morning, floor. I'm ready to start the day!"

Humming cheerfully, Emmet hunted through his books. "Ah, here it is!" He pulled the book

down and read its title aloud: "*Instructions to Fit In, Have Everybody Like You, and Always Be Happy.*"

Emmet turned to the first step and prepared to follow directions.

Step 1: Breathe.

"Okay," Emmet said, breathing deeply. "Got that one down." He opened the window and gazed out over his glorious city, Bricksburg.

Step 2: Greet the day, smile, and say, "Good morning, city!"

"Good morning, city!" Emmet cried happily. Shouts of "Good morning, city!" could be heard coming from all the other Minifigures who lived nearby.

Step 3: Exercise.

Emmet began to do jumping jacks, shouting, "Jumping jacks—hit 'em! One, two, three . . . I am so pumped up!"

Step 4: Shower.

Emmet hummed as he scrubbed up. As the soap bubbled around him, Emmet reminded

himself, "Always be sure to keep the soap out of your eye*ahhhh!*"

Step 5: Shave your face.
Step 6: Brush your teeth.
Step 7: Comb your hair.
Step 8: Wear clothes.

"Oops," Emmet giggled. "Almost forgot that one." He snapped on a surgeon's scrubs and shook his head. "No." Then he tried a Robin Hood costume. "Nuh-uh."

After testing out a scuba suit and a clown costume, Emmet finally found the perfect outfit—his construction worker's uniform. "And that's it! Check."

Step 9: Eat a complete breakfast with all the special people in your life.

Emmet turned to his houseplant. "Hey, Plantie, what do you want to do this morning, watch TV? Me too!"

Emmet clicked on the TV. He was just in time to catch President Business making an important announcement:

"Hi, I'm President Business, president of the Octan Corporation and the world. Let's take

extra care to follow the instructions, or you'll be put to sleep." Emmet chewed his waffles. "And don't forget, Taco Tuesday's coming next week! That's the day every rule-following citizen gets a free taco and *my love*. Have a great day, everybody!"

"You have a great day, too, President Business! Man, he's such a cool guy. I always want to hear more of what . . ." Emmet paused. "Wait, did he say 'put to sleep'?"

Before he could puzzle over the president's speech, Emmet's attention was drawn back to the TV. A commercial for his favorite show was on. "Tonight, on *Where Are My Pants?* . . ."

Emmet rolled around, laughing so hard at the scene on TV that he fell off the couch. Then he scratched his head. "What was I just thinking? Oh well, I don't care."

He headed out into Bricksburg, ready to face the day with a great big smile.

Step 10: Greet your neighbors.

"Good morning, Joe!" Emmet waved.

Joe the plumber jogged by with his handy wrench. "Hey, guy," he sang out.

"Hey, Surfer Dave." Emmet greeted a dude loading his surfboard onto his truck.

"Hey, brah," Surfer Dave replied.

Emmet grinned at one of his favorite neighbors. "Oh, good morning, Sherry."

"Hey, fella," Sherry answered. She was an odd lady with cats crawling all over her body.

Emmet said hello to each of the cats. "Oh, hey, Jasmine, Dexter, Angie, Loki, Bad Leroy, Fluffy, Fluffy Junior, Fluffy Senior, Jeff . . ."

The cats all meowed back at him as they scrambled into Sherry's car.

Emmet climbed into his car and pulled away from the curb.

Step 11: Turn on the radio and enjoy popular music.

He clicked on the radio. The super-popular pop song "Everything Is Awesome" came blasting from the speakers.

"Oh my gosh, I love this song!" Emmet gushed. He bobbed to the beat as he drove through town.

Emmet beamed as he watched his neighbors going about their day. Everyone was happy, and everyone was following the rules.

Always use a turn signal.
Park between the lines.
Drop off dry cleaning before noon.

Read the headlines.
Don't forget to smile.
Always root for the local sports team.

"Go, Sports Team!" everyone in Bricksburg shouted together.

Always return a compliment.

"Hey, you look nice," Emmet told a passerby.
"So do you!" the passerby replied.

Drink overpriced coffee.

"Here you go." Larry the coffee-shop barista pushed a sludgy cup of morning joe across the counter. "That's thirty-seven dollars."

Emmet flashed him a big smile of thanks. "Awesome!"

At the construction site, Emmet parked his car and ambled over to where the rest of the crew had gathered. Everyone was gaping up at a wall covered in graffiti.

Emmet scratched his head and read the graffiti aloud. "'Question Authority.' *Huh.*"

As Emmet spoke, representatives of the authority appeared at his side and removed the graffiti.

"Did you see *Where Are My Pants?* last night?" one of Emmet's co-workers asked.

"So funny," another co-worker replied. "Yes!"

"It was even funnier the second time."

"Where are my *paaaants*?"

Emmet laughed along with them. "Where are my *paaaants*?" he shouted. But, like always, he was a little late on the joke.

The whole crew headed into the construction site to start on that day's building instructions.

"Instructions coming in from Central!" Emmet's co-worker Barry announced. Sure enough, a set of rolled-up instructions was whooshing through a delivery tube in the middle of the construction clearing. "Okay, it says here to take everything weird and blow it up!"

The foreman, Frank, clapped his hands. "All right, cylinder-heads. Let's make it look exactly like it does on the cover!" He studied the LEGO instruction booklet, and then flipped to step one. "I need a two-by-four with some ball bearings up here. Come on, everybody, let's go!"

Emmet lifted his arm in the air and waved a 2 x 4 block around. "I got it!"

Frank nodded. "We need a two-by-two over here!"

Emmet found another piece and lifted it. "Two-by-two flying in!"

"Next I need a two-by-two transfer with frost doors on the line and two vertical lines on each side!"

"Roger that, Roger!" Emmet said, hunting for the piece.

The foreman looked panicked as he stared at the instructions. "Two-by-fours. Two-by-fours! Come on, everybody!"

Emmet whooped. "Two two-by-fours coming through!"

"Can I get a one-by-two keyhole?" Gail asked.

"Got it!" cried Emmet.

Wally yelled, "Can I get a jumper plate over here?"

"Here it is!" Emmet said happily.

"Now drill it down," Wally said.

Emmet scuttled around the site, gathering up everything the crew needed. His very favorite thing on earth was helping people follow the instructions for building perfect new buildings. "Here it is!"

As they worked, everyone sang their favorite song:

Everything is awesome!
Everything is cool when you're part of a team.
Everything is awesome!

Everyone felt great about their lives, their jobs, their *everything*. Because everything in Bricksburg *was* awesome. Perfectly built, organized, and orderly.

"Man," Emmet said, resting his hands on his hips, "I feel so good right now. I could sing this song for hours!"

And he did. At the end of the workday, Emmet joined the rest of the gang as they shuffled off the construction lot. The workers all sang "Everything Is Awesome" as they headed home for the night.

Everything is awesome!
Everything is cool when you're part of a team.
Everything is awesome!
We're living our dream.

"I'm going out after work tonight," Frank said, turning to the rest of the crew. "Who wants to eat some delicious chicken wings and get *craaaaazy*?"

"Chicken wings?!" Emmet yelped. "I love chicken wings!"

"Who wants to share a croissant with this guy?" Wally suggested.

"Croissants?!" Emmet shouted, his mouth watering. "I love croissants!"

"I sure do love giant sausages!" Barry added, joining the rest of the gang.

Emmet was absolutely thrilled, but no one seemed to notice his enthusiasm. He tried to weasel his way into the group. "Giant sausages! No way. You know, what I love to do is share giant sausages with the special people in my life. Frank? Wally? Gail? Me and you?" Emmet reached out for a high five. As he did, the instruction manual for that day's work blew right out of his hands!

"Ah, no, wait. Guys, wait up!" he yelled after the others, but no one seemed to notice that he'd fallen behind. "Okay," he called after them. "I'll meet you there."

Emmet clambered over a pile of construction debris, eager to find his instruction manual. He didn't want to get left behind and miss out on all the fun.

"What do I do? I wish I could remember the instructions for when I lose my instructions," Emmet muttered. Finally, he spotted the manual on a pile of rubble. "There you are!"

Suddenly, there was a *whoosh* behind him, and Emmet stood up straight. "I think I heard a *whoosh*."

He turned and saw a figure rummaging around in the rubble. Emmet had never seen this person before. It didn't look like anyone who worked on the crew.

"Hey, pal," Emmet called. "I hate to tell you this, but I don't think you're supposed to be here." Emmet referred to his instruction manual. "Yeah, the rules specifically state: Work site closes at six. This is a hard-hat area only — that's not official

safety orange. If you see anything weird, report it immediately—"

He pulled out his cell phone. "Well, I guess I'm going to have to report *youuuuuuuuuuuuuu*. . . ." Emmet's voice trailed off. The figure had pulled off its jacket hood, revealing herself to be the most spectacularly gorgeous girl he'd ever seen. Her hair framed her face like a halo, and it seemed to flutter in the breeze—even though there wasn't any breeze. She had long, lush dark eyelashes, a spattering of cute freckles, and plump, rosy lips. She was a knockout.

Emmet was speechless. He couldn't stop staring at her.

Suddenly, the strange and beautiful girl noticed him standing there. She turned and ran.

"Hey!" Emmet yelped. "Where are you going? Miss! I'm sorry, I didn't mean to scare you. . . ."

He chased after her, but before he'd gone more than a few steps, he tripped on a loose brick. "*Yaaow! Ow. Ow. Ow.*" He tumbled headfirst to the ground. As his face hit the pavement, it shattered beneath him. Emmet fell straight through!

3

"*AAAAAAAAAAAAAHHHHHHHHHHH!*" Emmet screamed as he bounced and bumped down a long, cavelike tunnel. "*Aaaahhh! Oof ow ee ah oof! Argh! Ow,* my back! *Owee, ouch!*"

He landed in a cave with a *thud*. It was almost entirely black inside, but there was a strange red glow coming from somewhere. "What is that?" Emmet said.

The object looked like a magical treasure — and also kind of like a red plastic rectangle. But that glow! Emmet was entranced by the way it glimmered, especially the bits of gooey crystal that surrounded its outer edges.

Emmet studied the object. He was strangely drawn to it, almost as if he were in a trance. But it was strange, and strange was dangerous. Still . . .

"I feel like maybe I should touch that."

Before he could stop it, Emmet's hand slowly reached out and touched the glowing red treasure.

A bright white light shot into the sky, and Emmet's world went dark.

Emmet slowly came around to the sound of an unfamiliar voice. "Wakey-wakey. Come on, wake up! Where are the Master Builders? How did you find the Piece of Resistance? Where are the others hiding?"

Emmet yawned and opened his eyes, wiping one hand across his face to brush away memories of a bad dream. "Good morning, apartment."

He was strapped to a chair in a stark interrogation room. A police officer stood in front of him, looking evil and impatient. He was one of those Bad Cops, the kind Emmet preferred to avoid.

Bad Cop got into Emmet's face. His breath smelled foul as he shouted, "Wake up! How did

you find the Piece of Resistance?"

Emmet turned away. "The piece of what?" he muttered groggily.

"The Piece of Resistance!" Bad Cop barked.

"Where am I? What's happening?" Emmet asked in confusion.

"'*Ooh* . . . what's happening?' Playing dumb, Master Builder?" Bad Cop mocked him.

"No," Emmet replied. "I—Master Builder?"

"Oh, so you've never heard of the prophecy . . . ?"

Emmet shook his head. "No."

"Or the Special . . . ?"

"No, no, I—"

"You're a liar!" Bad Cop shouted. He threw a chair across the room.

"Look, I watch a lot of cop shows on TV," Emmet said. "Isn't there supposed to be a Good Cop, too? If so, I'd like to talk to him."

"Oh, yes. But we're not done yet." Bad Cop spun his head around to reveal a Good Cop face he'd been hiding on the back.

"Hi, buddy!" Good Cop said warmly. He smiled at Emmet, and Emmet relaxed slightly. "I'm your friendly neighborhood police officer. Would you like a glass of water?"

Emmet grinned. "Yeah, actually, that sounds gre—"

The police officer's head swung around to

his Bad Cop face again. He knocked the glass of water Good Cop had given Emmet out of his hands. "Too bad! Security cameras picked up this." He pressed a button on a remote control, and a big TV rolled footage of Emmet's strange behavior at the construction site. "*Boom!* You were found convulsing with a strange piece."

"Yikes! That's disgusting!" Emmet yelped.

"Then why is it permanently stuck to your back?" Bad Cop demanded.

Emmet spun around to look at his back. That's when he realized the glowing red object from the creepy cave was now stuck to him. *"Ahhh!"* he squealed. "Get it off me! Get it off me! *Ahh!* It won't come off . . . it's chasing me!" Emmet bounced around on his chair, trying to get the piece off. "Look, it's not my fault. I have no idea how this thing got on my back."

Bad Cop turned into Good Cop again. "Of course, buddy! I believe you."

Emmet breathed a sigh of relief. "Great."

But then Bad Cop was back! "I 'believe' you, too. You see the quote marks I'm making with my claw hands? It means I *don't* believe you. Why else would you show up with that thing on your back just three days before President Business is going to use the Kragle to end the world?"

"President Business is going to end the world?!

But he's such a good guy," Emmet protested. "And Octan, his awesome company, they make good stuff: gas stations, music, dairy products, gas stations, coffee, TV shows, surveillance systems, history books, voting machines. . . . Wait a minute . . ."

Bad Cop stared at Emmet. "Oh, come on! You can't be this stupid."

"This is a misunderstanding! I'm just a regular, normal, ordinary guy," Emmet explained. "And I'm late to meet my best friends in the whole world—and they're probably missing me right now. They're probably out looking around, saying, 'Hey, where's Emmet?' and 'Hey, where's my best friend, Emmet?' You know what? Ask all my friends; they'll tell you."

"Oh, we asked them all right." Bad Cop snickered. *"Boom!"* He flicked on the TV again, and Emmet watched as Bad Cop ran video of interviews with his friends:

"Who is that guy? He's been our co-worker for years? Huh . . . he's not really that memorable."

"See?" Emmet said.

"You know, he's kind of an average, normal kind of guy."

Emmet grinned at his pal Wally on the screen. "Thank you, Wally."

Wally continued:

"Like, really normal. Like, we all blend in, but that guy really *does."*

Emmet scratched his head. That kind of stung. Then he watched as Gail — his good pal Gail — was interviewed:

"Wait, I'm so confused. Who are we talking about? Wait, does he work with us?"

Then Wally broke in:

"Look at Barry here. He likes sausage. That's something! Gail is perky. That's something. And Wally, well —"

Emmet's stomach felt queasy. These were his pals, his gang, his crew! Then his foreman, Frank, came on-screen:

"When you say Harry, I go — 'Ha, ha! *That guy's funny.' When you say the other guy — what'd you say, Emmet? — I go . . .* 'Huh?'"

Emmet slouched in his chair.

Surfer Dave came on-screen. Emmet waved to the TV as Surfer Dave said:

"I know that guy, but I know, like, zippy-zap about him."

"We just talked earlier!" Emmet muttered, thinking back to that morning. He and Surfer Dave had had a moment! They were brahs, buds, dudes. Frank broke in again:

"I mean, all he does is say yes to everything everybody else is doing."

Then Larry the barista came on-screen.

"He's just sort of a . . . a little bit of a blank slate, I guess."

Even Sherry had something to contribute.

"He's half as interesting as my least interesting cat."

Barry appeared again.

"We all have something that makes us something and Emmet is . . . nothing."

Emmet felt like he could cry. "There you go," he sighed as Bad Cop watched him closely. "I told you I was a nobody."

"Exactly," Bad Cop agreed. "It's the perfect cover."

"Cover?! Cover for what?" Emmet asked.

"Aargh!" Bad Cop cried. "I can't break him! Take him to the melting chamber."

Two robot cops in helmets barged into the room. They grabbed Emmet and dragged him into the melting chamber. *"Ahhh! Ahhh!* You're going to melt me? Am I going to die?"

Bad Cop spun his head around to the smiley side. "You'll live. You'll be fine." Then his phone rang, and he turned back into Bad Cop again. "Hello, President Business! I have him right here, sir. Yes, we've told him he'll live so he doesn't try to escape. But, um, we're lying."

"Wait!" Emmet screeched. "What did you just say?"

4

Inside the melting room, Emmet really began to panic. Tight straps secured him to a rack. Emmet squirmed around, desperate to escape.

"Hold still!" One of the robot cops pulled a lever on the rack's control, activating a laser.

"Wait!" Emmet whined. "There's obviously been a mix-up here. You've got the wrong—" He was trapped facedown under the laser, which began to burn the area around the red piece. *"Ow ow ow ow. Ow!* That is gonna start hurting pretty soon!"

Suddenly, someone burst into the room. The mysterious figure zipped and zapped around, ninja-ing the police-robot dudes. Then it dashed over to Emmet, swinging an axe. Emmet winced, certain he was about to be chopped to bits. But instead, the figure broke off his chains, freeing him!

A siren went off and red lights began to flash.

"Whoa!" Emmet said in awe.

The figure pulled back its hood, and he realized it was the gorgeous girl who'd been poking around the construction site earlier! "It's you!"

"Come with me if you wanna not die," she told him.

She grabbed Emmet's hand, and the two of them ran toward the window.

A moment later, Good Cop strode in.

"Hey, everyone, how's the melting going?" Then he realized what had happened and immediately turned into Bad Cop. "Red alert! Red alert!" he screamed into his walkie-talkie. "I need everyone—repeat, EVERYONE—to go after the Special! And put his picture up all over the city!"

The girl jumped out the window without a moment's hesitation, but Emmet wasn't quite so sure. *"Ummmm . . ."* He peeked outside at the three-story jump. Then he took a deep breath and jumped after her. He bounced once on the fire

escape, and then landed headfirst in a trash can. "*Ow. Ugh! Ow*, my neck."

The girl ignored his pitiful escape skills. "The tunnel's that way. Oh, sir, you're brilliant. We'll build a motorcycle out of the alleyway."

"I tried to land there for that exact reason," Emmet said.

The girl yanked the roller shutter off a doorway and bent it into a circle. Then she tore apart a Dumpster and threw LEGO pieces around, building feverishly. "We'll need this, this, need this . . . over here." She threw pieces together without thinking about it.

"So, uh, I didn't catch your name or anything, or anything about what you're doing or what we're up to here," Emmet said. He had never seen someone build without instructions before. And so quickly!

"It's brilliant, sir, that you pretended to be a useless nobody, but you can drop the act with me. It's cool," the girl said.

"Oh, the act?" Emmet said, puzzled. *"Whoa!"*

The girl had finally completed her creation. She stepped aside to reveal the fastest, most ferocious motorcycle Emmet had ever seen. She hopped on and revved the engine.

"All right. That doesn't scare me that it's dangerous," Emmet said.

"Let's go!" The girl grabbed Emmet and tossed

him onto the back of the bike. They squealed out of the alley.

As they zoomed away, police cars peeled after them. "All units! Cut him off on Elm Street! Or whenever you can." Bad Cop was in the first police car, shouting into a walkie-talkie.

Motorcycle-Slash-Hero Girl drove faster.

"They're up on the monorail!" cried Bad Cop. "Release the copper choppers!"

No sooner had he spoken than a helicopter dropped two motorcycles onto a ramp right in front of Emmet and the motorcycle girl. The girl swerved their bike out of the way just in time.

"This is definitely not an approved driver lane," Emmet shouted.

The girl didn't answer. She steered off the rail onto the freeway. The cops' motorcycles weren't so lucky. They smashed into an oncoming train.

"There's a speed limit and you're going *wayyyyy* over it right now!" Emmet cried.

The girl barely blinked. "We need to meet up with Vitruvius and tell him the Piece has been found."

"Uh-huh," Emmet said. "Will you please tell me what's happening?"

Emmet glanced back and swallowed a tiny bit of throw-up—there were another two police motorcycles popping wheelies behind them, and a chopper hovered in the air above them. When

he looked up, he spotted his picture plastered on a huge Jumbotron, with the word *WANTED* underneath it.

"I'm rescuing you, sir," the girl shouted through the roar of the chase. "You're the one the prophecy spoke of. You're the Special."

"Me?" Emmet gasped.

"You found the Piece of Resistance," she said. She spoke confidently as she maneuvered the motorcycle toward the outskirts of the city. "And the prophecy states that you are the most important, most talented, most interesting, and most extraordinary person in the universe. That's you, right?"

Emmet swallowed. "Uh, yeah." No one had ever said anything half so nice about him before. And now here was the most beautiful girl in the world talking about him like he was the most amazing person in all of Bricksburg! He didn't know what to say. "That's me," he managed to say. "Who is . . . all those things you just said."

She smiled. "Great. Then you drive." The girl shot a grappling hook onto a street sign overhead, then swung off the bike. As she somersaulted through the air, she took out the copper chopper. A moment later, she landed gracefully on a robot cop's bike, casually pushing the driver away as she took control.

"What?!" Emmet was left holding the wheel of the motorcycle. "Oh my gosh. *Aahhh!* Okay, I don't know what I'm doing."

Emmet gripped the handlebars, knocking over one of the police motorcycles out of sheer luck. Motorcycle Girl was busy fighting the robot cops pursuing them.

Emmet squeezed his eyes closed tightly, before remembering that he—plain, old Emmet—was driving a motorcycle! He tried to steer on his own. "Okay. Oh, sorry. Sorry! *Ahhhh* . . . I wanna go home!"

When he opened his eyes again, he realized he was driving straight into a house being towed behind a truck. "*Ahhhh!* That's not what I meant!" he cried as he crashed right through it.

Panicked, Emmet clutched the handlebars even tighter. Suddenly, he and his bike were doing a front wheelie—and the next thing he knew, he was zipping along the highway, knocking over pursuers right and left.

"*Whoa,*" Emmet said, watching in shock as a police car slammed into a wall.

The crazy girl zoomed up beside him and hopped onto the back of the cycle again. Emmet tried to focus, but it was hard when a team of robots was firing lasers at them.

"Wow! That was incredible," Motorcycle Girl

said. "You're even better than the prophecy said you'd be."

"Uh, thanks," Emmet said.

"I — I'm Wyldstyle."

"I'm sorry, what?" Emmet shouted.

"Wyldstyle," she repeated.

"Wyldstyle?"

"Yep," the girl replied.

"Cool. Are you, like, a DJ or something?"

"No."

Emmet considered this. "Is that your real name?"

"Let's not talk about my name."

"It's hard not to, 'cause your name is *Wyldstyle*," Emmet said.

Before Wyldstyle could respond, Bad Cop's voice rang out behind them. "Don't let the Special get away!"

A police blockade was set up in the middle of the road in front of them. "Hang on, sir!" Wyldstyle shouted. In an instant, she transformed their motorcycle into a moto-plane, and they shot up into the sky. "Head for the secret tunnel!"

"These are the city limits!" Emmet cried, gulping.

But sure enough, just ahead of them there was a portal in the wall of the city. It was spinning with weird, brightly colored pieces and mystery bits.

"Let's just head for the tunnel." Wyldstyle leaned out and fired at the robots and Bad Cop, who were racing after them in a fleet of police cars.

"I can't do this! It's against the instructions," Emmet said.

Wyldstyle stared openmouthed, finally noticing Emmet's cowardice. "Wait . . . what's your favorite restaurant?"

"Any chain restaurant," Emmet answered.

"Favorite TV show?"

"*Where Are My Pants?* Ha."

Wyldstyle cringed. "Favorite song?"

"'Everything Is Awesome'!"

"Oh, no . . ." Wyldstyle looked horrified.

"Ahhhhh!" Emmet screamed and closed his eyes as they crashed into the tunnel. It immediately closed behind them. The plane began to disintegrate as Emmet and Wyldstyle tumbled through a maze of tunnels.

Bad Cop and his gang of robots were left behind in Bricksburg. And Bad Cop was furious about it.

Sensing Bad Cop's frustration, a robot cop handed him a chair to throw. Bad Cop began kicking it around. "Darn darn darn darny darn DARN!" He flung the chair away, taking out a few robots along with it.

5

Wyldstyle led Emmet through a twisty tunnel. At the end, they both fell out and straight into . . . the Old West. Emmet bounced painfully down a rock face, while Wyldstyle slid smoothly along beside him.

"Where are we?" asked Emmet, picking himself up off the ground. Above him, the words *THE OLD WEST!* floated in the air. Covered wagons ambled by, and a pack of horses and their riders galloped past. "This is so weird."

Wyldstyle threw a cactus at him. "You're not the Special!" she hissed. "You lied to me."

"Well," Emmet said, trying to act cool, which was difficult since he was still wincing in pain. "Well, I mean, it . . . it really kind of depends on —"

"You're not even a Master Builder, are you?"

"Uh, I mean, I know what a Master Builder is, but why don't you do me a favor. Why don't you tell me what it is? That way I can see if you're right. . . ."

Wyldstyle lunged at him and tried to pry the Piece of Resistance off his back. "You ruined the prophecy!"

Emmet pushed her away. "I'm sorry, okay? You just—you made being special sound so good."

"And to think that I was going to follow you to the end of the universe," said Wyldstyle despairingly.

"You were?" Emmet said softly. "Well, uh, here's the thing. How do we know for sure that I'm *not* the Special? We just don't know it yet. . . ."

Suddenly, Wyldstyle looked alert. "Quiet!" She pulled Emmet behind a rock. Two cowboys were nearby, leaning against a covered wagon.

"Y'all want a giant turkey leg?" the first cowboy asked.

"Do you have any idea what that does to your colon?" his partner replied.

Before Emmet even realized she was gone,

Wyldstyle had leaped out from behind the rock and head-butted the two cowboys.

"Oh my gosh, is that necessary?" Emmet demanded.

Wyldstyle ignored him. She was rummaging through the cowboys' wagon and digging out supplies. She pulled out an old-fashioned dress with a corset and put it on. "Just put this hat on. Oh, and this. And this. And this. And this." The last item she tossed at him was a horse, which flattened him.

Emmet struggled to his feet. Then he shrugged, pulling a poncho over the Piece of Resistance. Next he added a mustache and a cowboy hat.

"And by the way, I have a *boyfriend*."

"U-uhhh," Emmet stuttered. "I don't, uhhh . . . I'm not sure exactly why you'd bring that up."

"It's super serious and you do not want to mess with him. So don't get any ideas," Wyldstyle warned him, hopping on her horse.

"I never have any ideas." Emmet pouted as he clumsily climbed onto his own horse. "Hey, listen. Um, can you explain to me, like, why I'm dressed like this, and what those big words in the sky were all about, and where we are . . . in . . . uh, time?"

Wyldstyle tugged at her horse's reins. Both she and her horse rolled their eyes. "Bricksburg—where you live—is one of many realms in the

universe. There's also this one—the Old West—Viking's Landing, Clown Town, and a bunch of others we don't need to mention."

"Uh-huh," said Emmet, trying to follow.

"It was once a glorious time in all the realms," Wyldstyle continued. "There was freedom and joy and buildsmanship, and we were all so happy. But Lord Business was intimidated by all this free mixing of people and ideas. He didn't understand that pirates and ninja could hang out together. Or that robots and cavemen could learn from one another. So he erected walls between all the worlds, and he hired Bad Cop to hunt all the Master Builders. Those of us who remain, we went into hiding, and we built the tunnels to survive."

"Ohh-kay," said Emmet.

"Lord Business, or—as you think you know him—President Business, stole the Kragle," Wyldstyle went on. "The Kragle is the most powerful object in the universe."

"Uh-huh. Yes. Got it." Emmet squinted at Wyldstyle. He was trying really hard to follow, but all he heard was, "Blah blah blah blah proper name. Place name, backstory stuff. *I'm pretty!* Blah blah, and I'm angry at you for some reason."

Wyldstyle continued with her explanation, unaware that Emmet was zoning out. "The only

thing that can stop the Kragle is the Piece of Resistance, and according to Vitruvius's prophecy, whoever finds it is the Special. The Special is supposed to unite the remaining Master Builders into an army, lead them to storm Lord Business's Octan Office Tower at the end of the universe, put the Piece of Resistance onto the Kragle, and disarm it forever."

Emmet nodded. "Great. I think I got it, but just in case, tell me the whole thing again? I wasn't listening."

They had reached Main Street. Wyldstyle sighed and dismounted. She pulled out some flash cards to make her presentation as simple as possible. "Kragle, bad. Prophecy, good. Go to office tower. Put thing on other thing. Save world."

"Kragle . . . I've heard of that. Oh!" Emmet gasped. "That cop was talking about the Kragle. He said in three days, President Business is going to use the Kragle to end the world!"

Wyldstyle couldn't believe it. "Taco Tuesday! I knew that was suspicious. There's no time to lose. We must find Vitruvius and get to the office tower before it's too late!"

Emmet shrugged. "How scary can someone's office be?"

6

The Octan Office Tower, Lord Business's headquarters, was undoubtedly the scariest office tower in the universe. It was a hulking building that jutted out over a chasm and seemed to rise into space and beyond. It dangled over an immense cavern of nothingness that led to the end of the universe.

Robot workers shuffled paperwork and answered phones in bland cubicles lined up side by side. As President Business made his way through the corridors, robots approached him with memos to sign.

"Hey, guys," he said. "Great job selling Taco Tuesday. And remember, don't call it Doomsday Tuesday. That's too depressing. Just say Taco Tuesday."

President Business headed through the Radio Department, bobbing his head along to "Everything Is Awesome," which was blasting over the airwaves.

"Everything will be awesome on Taco Tuesday if you keep playing this song on an endless loop so it will bore into everyone's brains and make them lose their free will, okay?" He gave the robo DJs a cheesy fist pump. "Thanks, you're the best!"

As President Business strolled past the TV Department, the cast and crew of *Where Are My Pants?* were just wrapping up another day on set.

"Honey, where are my *paaaaants*?" The lead actor milked his last line as the robots in the audience roared with programmed laughter.

"And—" the show's director began.

President Business shoved the director aside and shouted, "Cut! Wonderful. I have a few thoughts." He sized up the leading lady. "Sharon, I think your hair is really distracting. Let's get her a new wig." He glanced at the lead actor. "And, Blake, I don't think you even care where your pants are. Great job, everyone. Good-bye!"

A security robot approached him. "President Business," it droned, "we are trying to locate the fugitive, Emmet Brickowski, but his face is so generic it matches every other face in our database."

"Diabolical," President Business seethed.

President Business's robot assistant followed him. "Bad Cop is waiting for you in your office, sir."

"Wonderful. Could you cancel my two o'clock? This next meeting might run a little deadly," President Business replied.

As he strode down a long corridor, a computerized voice began to issue instructions. "Initiate transformation sequence from President Business to Lord Business." President Business stepped onto a platform, and his legs connected to two enormous lifts that grew even taller as he stomped along.

"Deploy cape," the computer continued. "We are go for shoulder harness. Activate helmet." A helmet, cape, and chest plate were lowered down from the ceiling and locked into place.

"Smoke-and-light sequence initiated," the computer went on. Smoke billowed from the horns of his helmet as his leg-lifts pulsed with terrifying red light. Within moments, the transformation to Lord Business was complete.

"Lord Business is ready. Go for two o'clock

meeting. I repeat, we are go for two o'clock meeting."

Lord Business burst through the doors of his relic room with a flourish.

The room was filled with human treasures that looked monstrous and strange inside their LEGO world. A human thumbtack, a giant eraser, a gum wrapper, and other incredible items were displayed on pedestals around the room.

"Bad Cop." Lord Business greeted Bad Cop with a curt nod.

"Lord Business, I know the Special got away, but I—I—" Bad Cop stammered.

"Don't be so serious!" Lord Business said gently. "Where's the other guy?"

Bad Cop swiveled his head around, and Good Cop smiled back at Lord Business. "Hey!"

Lord Business grinned back. "Hey, buddy. I missed you!"

"*Aww,* did you really?" said Good Cop.

Lord Business's smile didn't falter, but there was something sinister about the way he looked at Good Cop when he said, "Have I ever shown you my relic collection?"

Good Cop swallowed nervously. "Nope, I don't think you have."

"Nobody knows where this stuff comes from." Lord Business glanced around the relic room,

admiring his treasures. He picked up a dirty Band-Aid and held it up. "This one is the Cloak of Ban Da'Id. I hear it's super painful to take off. You want to try it on?"

"No, but thank you." Good Cop turned his face back to Bad Cop again. Bad Cop was better at dealing with Lord Business. Good Cop just wanted to run away whenever Lord Business looked at him.

Lord Business tossed the Band-Aid to the ground. "We've done some great work over the years together, Bad Cop. Capturing all those Master Builders and torturing them and whatnot."

"Thank you, sir." Bad Cop was nervous.

"But the thing is, you did let the Piece of Resistance go. . . ." Lord Business frowned. "The one thing that can ruin my plans. The one thing that I asked you to take care of. That's super frustrating." He lifted Bad Cop by the back of his neck and carried him over to a window overlooking a swirling, infinite nothingness. He squished Bad Cop's face up against it. "It makes me want to pick up whoever is standing closest to me and just throw them through this window and out into the infinite abyss." He leaned in closer to Bad Cop and whispered, "I wanna do it so bad."

Bad Cop quivered. "Yes, sir. I know you do, sir. But please don't."

"It's not just you that keeps messing up my plans, Bad Cop," Lord Business said, dropping him. "People everywhere are always messing with my stuff. But I have a way to fix that, and keep things the way they're supposed to be permanently. The most powerful weapon of all the relics." He pushed a button, and a strange object appeared on a giant display screen. "Behold! The power of the Kragle! *THE KRAGLE!*"

Lord Business admired his most powerful weapon—a tube of Krazy Glue, with some of the letters rubbed off. It now simply said:

KRA GL E

"As you can see, they're loading the Kragle in a big machine upstairs I call the Kraglizer. It's going to spray the Kragle all over everyone and everything with a bunch of super-scary nozzles, like this one." He pressed another button, and a huge mechanical tentacle emerged from a secret panel in the ceiling. "I'll show you how it works."

"Sir, I don't know that this is necessary. . . ." Bad Cop said hastily.

"Oh, don't worry," Lord Business said. "I won't test it on you, I'll test it on your parents!"

Suddenly, the floor opened up, and a platform rose to their level. On the platform were Bad Cop's

parents, standing in front of a quaint country cottage.

Bad Cop's dad waved at him eagerly. "Hiya, son! How's it goin' in the big city?"

"Mommy? Daddy?" Bad Cop tried not to let his voice shake. "What are you doing here?"

"Okay, Pa, I just want you to act naturally," Lord Business said. "Like a small-time loser with no ambition or real purpose in life."

Pa Cop beamed. "Gotcha."

Lord Business rubbed his hands together. "Yeah, keep your hand up like that. Ma, scoot two steps in to the right. Pa, why is it that whenever I talk to Ma, you start to move? Get back to where you were!"

Pa Cop shuffled. "Oh, sorry. Here?" He glanced up for approval. "Right?"

Lord Business nodded. "Perfect. Great. You can't do anything better. There's no reason why you should move. Now, Ma, hand on his shoulder. And, Pa, you just moved—and you just wrecked it again! YOU WRECKED IT!"

Lord Business turned to Bad Cop. "You see what I'm talking about? All I'm asking for is TOTAL PERFECTION!" He sighed. "Send in a micromanager."

A scary black robot with long arms entered. "Commencing micromanagement," it droned. Its

long arms reached out and repositioned Ma and Pa Cop.

"Hold still, you guys!" Lord Business said. "Pow!" He pointed the mechanical tentacle at Ma and Pa Cop and pulled a lever. The tentacle instantly zapped their feet with a thick, gooey spray. Ma and Pa were glued in place!

Ma Cop looked panicked. "Oh, Pa—hold me."

"Oh, darling," Pa Cop said. "I can't move—my legs."

Bad Cop tried to stay calm, but Lord Business got in his face and egged him on. "Does that upset you, Bad Cop?"

"Um . . ." Bad Cop didn't want to look at Lord Business lest his boss see that it did, in fact, upset him.

"Surely you feel bad for your parents, and you want to help them, don't you?"

"We're okay, son," Pa Cop piped up. "Just a little stuck, is all."

"Go ahead," Lord Business urged, holding the Kraglizer remote out to Bad Cop. "Finish the job." He put Bad Cop's hand over the button and repositioned the spray arm so it was pointing straight at Ma's and Pa's heads.

"Of course, sir," said Bad Cop. He felt sick with indecision. His face spun from Bad Cop to Good Cop. "No, I don't want to," Good Cop whispered.

His face spun back to Bad Cop. "You have to . . ." he muttered to himself.

Then Good Cop was back. "I don't want to . . ." he whimpered.

But Bad Cop took over a moment later. "Would you please be quiet?"

"I can't . . ." said Good Cop.

"You must!" Bad Cop commanded.

"But it's not nice. . . ." Good Cop protested.

"It's your job!" Bad Cop insisted.

Good Cop shuddered. "I can't do it. They're innocent."

"Just as I thought," Lord Business scoffed. "Your Good Cop side is making you soft, Bad Cop." He called out, "Robots, bring me the Fleece-Crested Scepter of Q-Teep and the Po-Lish Remover of Na'll."

Then he turned his attention back to Bad Cop. "You've already let the Special get away once. I'm going to make sure it doesn't happen again."

His robots marched in with a human-sized Q-tip and a bottle of nail polish remover. They held Bad Cop down and twisted his face around.

As Good Cop struggled to escape, Lord Business dipped the Q-tip in nail polish remover . . . and then wiped off Good Cop's face! "No more Mr. Nice Guy!"

"Oh, son," Ma Cop said, horrified.

Lord Business looked delighted. “On Taco Tuesday I am going to Kraglize the entire universe so it will be exactly how I like it. Are you gonna be with me? Or are you gonna be stuck having a *tea party with your mom and daddy*?!”

Bad Cop looked at his frozen parents with a cold expression on his face.

“Son?” Pa Cop whispered.

“Sorry, Dad. . . .” Bad Cop shrugged. “I have a job to do.”

Bad Cop pressed the button, and the Kragle shot clear liquid at his parents’ bodies. They stared blankly at him from inside their frozen, glue-gooped prison.

7

Back in the Old West, Emmet and Wyldstyle sauntered toward a lively saloon. "All you have to do is blend in and act like you belong here," Wyldstyle whispered.

"Ah, perfect," Emmet whispered back.

They entered the saloon. Emmet immediately turned and grinned at a few of the unsavory characters crowded around the bar. "Well, howdy!" he shouted. "I'm a cowboy! *Bang bang bang! Zap zap pow!*"

All the cowboys stopped and stared.

Wyldstyle hastily pulled Emmet back outside.

"What are they looking at?" Emmet wondered aloud.

"I made a mistake," Wyldstyle groaned. "You should just act like a stool. Just be still, okay?"

Emmet wandered back into the saloon and nodded at a few of the cowboys. "Howdy, guys. Come sit on me," he called, bending over onto all fours.

Wyldstyle called after him, "Quiet—nope. Stools don't talk." She pulled him outside again. "Let's play the quiet game, okay? *Shhh.*"

She returned to the bar, pulling Emmet along behind her. She spit into a spittoon, and everyone resumed their rowdiness. "Okay," she whispered to Emmet. "Let's just find the wizard and get this over with."

As they shuffled across the room, an Old West sheriff eyed them suspiciously. A bearded old man was playing piano in the corner, tinkling the notes of "Everything Is Awesome."

"Psst," Wyldstyle said, nudging Emmet. She pointed at the piano man, who was blind. "There he is." They made their way across the bar and stood beside the piano. "Vitruvius."

"Who?!" the piano man squawked. "I've never heard of that man, who I am not. Who are you?"

Wyldstyle leaned in to whisper. "It's me."

"I am a blind man and cannot see," said the piano man, continuing to play.

"Wyldstyle."

"Are you a DJ?" the old man asked.

"What?" Wyldstyle put her hands on her hips. "Why does everybody—"

"Oh, wait. Are you the student I used to have who was so insecure she kept changing her name?"

"No," Wyldstyle muttered, squaring her shoulders. "No . . ."

"Yeah, yeah . . . first Darkstorm, then Gemini, then Neversmile, then Freakface, then Snazzypants . . ."

"Okay, okay, I get it. Yes, fine, it's me," snapped Wyldstyle.

Vitruvius nodded. "Meet me upstairs in ten seconds."

Emmet and Wyldstyle hustled upstairs. Ten seconds later, they were following Vitruvius into his apartment.

"Whoa," Emmet said, looking around. "You have a very weirdly decorated place."

"Thank you," Vitruvius said.

Wyldstyle didn't have time for chitchat. "Vitruvius, we have found the Piece of Resistance."

Vitruvius sat on an upside-down chair attached to the ceiling. "Is it . . . true?"

"Yes, but—"

Vitruvius cut her off. "Wyldstyle, the prophecy

states that you are the Special. The embodiment of good. The foiler of evil. The most talented, most brilliant, most important person in the universe."

"That would be great," Wyldstyle grumbled. "But Emmet is the one who found the Piece."

Emmet smiled sheepishly.

"Oh, okay." Vitruvius shrugged. "Emmet, the prophecy states that YOU are the Special. The most talented, most brilliant, most important person in the universe."

Wyldstyle rolled her eyes. "I'm not sure he's the Special, actually, because he's not even a Master Builder. Watch. Emmet, just given what's around you, build something simple, like an awesome race car. Go!"

Emmet nodded. "Okay, great. Do you have the instructions?"

"You must create the instructions in your mind, my liege," Vitruvius coached.

"Huh." Emmet scratched his head. "Okay. Race car. Um, well, there is a lot of really cool stuff here. But I don't see a wheel or . . . three more wheels. . . ."

"See?" Wyldstyle protested. "He can't do it. He will never be a Master Builder."

"Of course not. Not if you keep telling him he can't. He needs to see that he can." Vitruvius

reached forward and plucked Emmet's hair off his head.

"What are you doing?" Emmet shrieked.

Vitruvius put his hands on Emmet's now bald Minifigure head. Wyldstyle sighed and joined him. "We are entering your mind to prove that you have the unlocked potential to be a Master Builder."

"Leave my hair on!" Emmet whined. He was *supposed* to have hair. He didn't look right bald.

Wyldstyle and Vitruvius focused on Emmet's head as he squirmed under their touch.

"*Ha-ha-ha,* that's weird. Oh, that tickles. Stop! *Hee-hee-hee* —"

A moment later, Emmet stopped giggling and opened his eyes. He was floating in the middle of a bleak, empty space.

"Wow," Wyldstyle mused. *"Mm-hmm."*

"Whoa!" Emmet looked around at the blankness that surrounded them. "Are we inside my brain right now? It's big. I must be smart."

"I'm not hearing a lot of activity here," Vitruvius said.

"I don't think he's ever had an original thought in his life." Wyldstyle sighed.

"*Ha-ha,* well, that's not true." Emmet considered this. "For instance, one time I wanted to have all my friends over to watch TV in my apartment, but my

apartment's too small. So I was like, what if there was a couch, but, like, a *bunk bed*. Introducing the double-decker couch! So everyone could watch TV together and be buddies!"

As Emmet spoke, a double-decker couch appeared in the air behind him.

Wyldstyle studied him, and then the couch. "That is literally the dumbest thing I've ever heard."

"Please, Wyldstyle, let me handle this," Vitruvius cut in. "That idea is just the worst. But with proper training you could become a great Master Builder."

"I could?" Emmet asked.

"The prophecy chose *you*, Emmet," Vitruvius said.

"But I can't do any of the stuff the prophecy says I'm supposed to do."

"All you have to do is discover what you already know," Vitruvius explained. "Then you will see everything. Are you ready, my son?"

"Yes, I am!" said Emmet. "I think . . ."

Wyldstyle walked away, muttering, "There's no time to train him. Lord Business is going to use the Kragle to end the world in three days."

"Then we haven't a moment to lose," Vitruvius declared. "We must assemble the Master Builders."

Meet Emmet Brickowski. He's just your average, everyday LEGO Minifigure . . .

EMMET
. . . until the day he stumbles into a hole at a construction site and discovers the legendary Piece of Resistance!

The next thing Emmet knows, he's being interrogated by Bad Cop . . .

. . . till a stunning and streetwise Master Builder named Wyldstyle comes to his rescue.

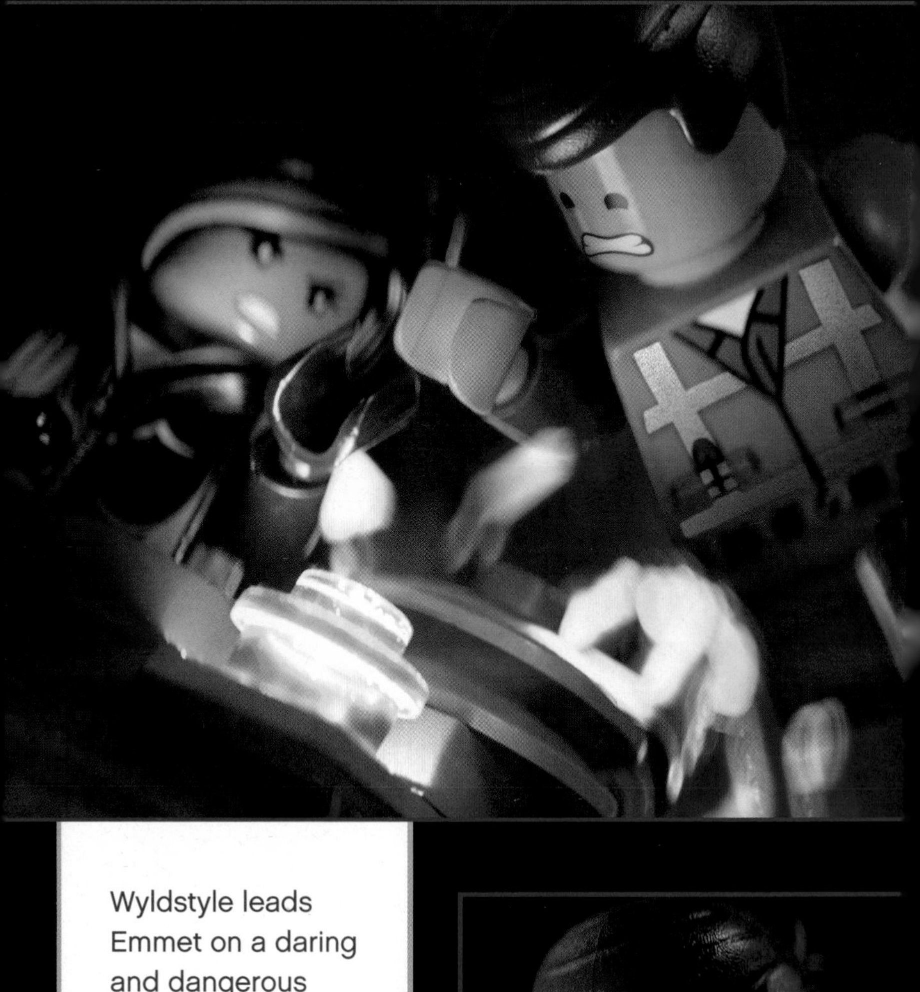

Wyldstyle leads Emmet on a daring and dangerous escape.

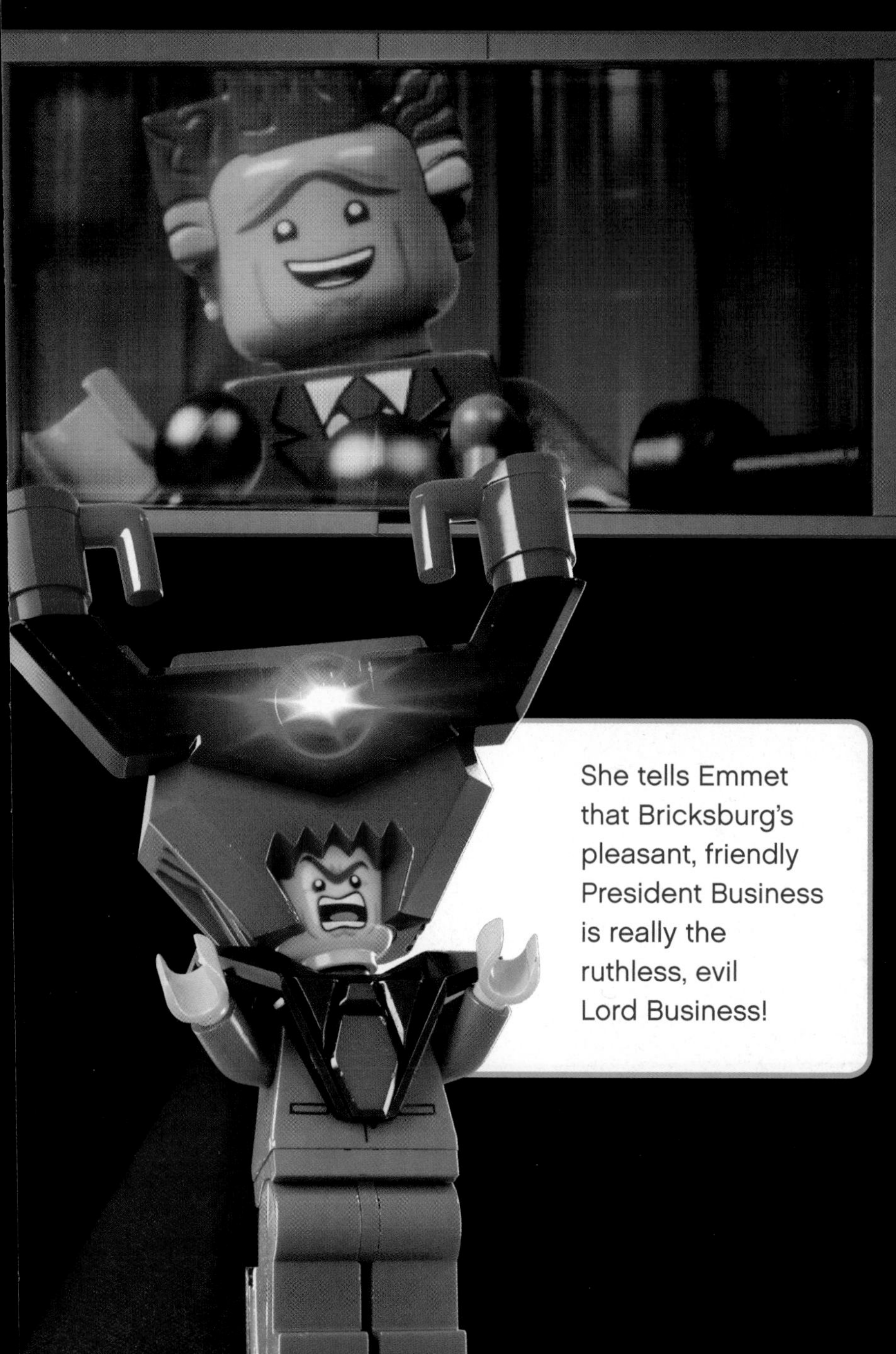

She tells Emmet that Bricksburg's pleasant, friendly President Business is really the ruthless, evil Lord Business!

KELLEY
Wyldstyle brings Emmet
to meet a wise wizard,
Vitruvius, in another LEGO
realm, the Old West . . .
WANTED!
. . . but Bad
Cop is hot
on their trail!

Emmet's mission is to unite the heroic Master Builders, including Superman, Abraham Lincoln, and Batman!

Does Emmet have what it takes to save the universe from Lord Business?

8

Back in the wizard's apartment, Vitruvius constructed a flock of birds and released them from the window. "These mechanical birds will get our message out," he explained. "They will go to an Internet café and e-mail the remaining Master Builders, who will meet us in the secret realm of Cloud Cuckoo Land."

"Cloud Cuckoo Land? I thought that place was a myth," Wyldstyle said.

"No, it really exists," Vitruvius assured her.

"Okay, cool, yeah—secret land," Emmet said.

"Um, I was wondering—when do I start learning how to be a Master Builder? 'Cause I'm not feeling super ready."

"Your training begins now," Vitruvius declared. "Lesson one: Look around you. All great ideas begin with observation."

Suddenly, someone knocked on the door. "Piano man? Sing us a song!"

Vitruvius sighed. "Your training begins later." Then he called, "Just a moment! I'm in my bra!"

"Oh, pardon me, ma'am," the voice outside the door said sheepishly. "Wait a minute . . . that's not a girl." There was a pause, then, "All right, on three. One . . ."

Before they got to three, the door to Vitruvius's apartment was blown to smithereens! Sheriff Not-a-Robot from the saloon downstairs rushed in, along with some other Old West riffraff.

Fortunately, Vitruvius, Emmet, and Wyldstyle had already escaped through a trapdoor in the ceiling. "Whew, I think we're in the clear," Wyldstyle said, climbing onto the roof of the saloon.

"Freeze, turkeys!" Bad Cop had tracked them down. He and his team of supersecret police robots had the whole place surrounded! Blasters were pointed at our heroes from every direction. "All I want is the Piece of Resistance," Bad Cop barked through his megaphone.

Wyldstyle shouted back, "We would rather he died than give it to you."

"Uh . . . I—I would not rather he died," Emmet stuttered.

Bad Cop waved his blaster at them. "Look, everybody, we can do this the easy way, or we can do it—"

But Wyldstyle didn't wait for the *or*. "Go! Run!" she shouted.

"They took the hard way!" Bad Cop groaned. "Fire! Fire!"

Blaster fire fell all around Emmet, Vitruvius, and Wyldstyle as they jumped onto a balcony and sprinted along the railing.

Bad Cop pulled out a megaphone and started barking instructions. Sheriff Not-a-Robot and hundreds of police robots chased after Emmet, Vitruvius, and Wyldstyle.

Wyldstyle led Emmet and Vitruvius onto the roof of the next building. As each section of roof ran out, Wyldstyle used her Master Builder skills to build more. Emmet and Vitruvius raced from roof to roof behind her.

"Vitruvius, which way to Cloud Cuckoo Land?" asked Wyldstyle, panting.

"Head for the big bright thing in the sky."

"You mean the sun?" Emmet asked.

"Yeah," Vitruvius said. "Yeah, that's it."

"We have to build our way out of here!" Wyldstyle yelled. "Come on!"

Things were getting desperate. On the roof behind them, Wyldstyle and Emmet could see a giant tower of robots stacking up. The robots bent over, creating a bridge between the roofs. Sheriff Not-a-Robot charged across the robots on horseback.

"Come on! Hurry!" Wyldstyle cried. "Let's get out of here!!!"

As they fled, Wyldstyle started building around Emmet. He had no clue what she was doing, but he kept running over roofs anyway.

When they reached the edge of the last rooftop, Emmet finally realized what Wyldstyle had created — a makeshift hang glider!

"Come on, let's fly!" Wyldstyle cried. She and Vitruvius clung to the wings as Emmet flung himself off the roof. He steered the glider clumsily. "I don't know what I'm doing!" he shrieked, trying not to panic.

Shots echoed all around them. Bad Cop had them in his sights! "I've got them!" he snarled, aiming a massive blaster at the glider.

Bad Cop's aim was true. The glider was destroyed with a single shot. It plummeted into the barrel of a water tower, which collapsed.

A moment later, a tidal wave of water exploded through town. Emmet, Vitruvius, and Wyldstyle were washed all the way down Main Street. Wyldstyle landed in a carpenter's workshop with a splash. Emmet and Vitruvius ended up facedown in a pigsty.

"Hey, where'd you guys go?" Wyldstyle shouted.

Emmet struggled to make his way through a mud pile and a pack of pigs. "*Arghh!* Got pigs!"

"Guys, quit playing around in the mud!" Wyldstyle cried. Emmet and Vitruvius could hear frantic building noises coming from the workshop where she'd landed. "I could really use your help."

"Wyldstyle, we could really use *your* help. Lotta pigs in here," Emmet replied. He stumbled toward the workshop and got tangled up in a load of rope fencing.

Before Emmet could untangle himself, Wyldstyle emerged from the carpenter's shed in another amazing creation—a wooden vehicle that looked like a high-speed sports car. She yanked on the ropes around Emmet's ankles, and in one swift motion she managed to harness the pigs, pull Emmet and Vitruvius onboard, and create reins for her new pig-powered wagon. They sped away with Bad Cop and legions of robo-police and robo-cowboys in hot pursuit.

Wyldstyle looked over her shoulder. Bad Cop was getting closer. "Vitruvius, they're gaining on us!" Wyldstyle yelled. "Build something!"

"Let Emmet try," Vitruvius suggested.

"Vitruvius, help me think of something!" Emmet pleaded.

"Master Builder training lesson number two: Trust your instincts!" Vitruvius responded.

Emmet looked around helplessly. "Uh, okay. Um . . . this. Take that!" He put two bricks together and tossed them behind him. They landed on the ground with a useless *thud*. Bad Cop and his robot minions trampled over them. Emmet's creation didn't slow their pursuers down even for an instant.

"Thanks," Wyldstyle groaned. "That was great."

"You put a lot of pressure on me, you know," Emmet told her.

Wyldstyle rolled her eyes. "Giddyup! Hi-yah!"

Sheriff Not-a-Robot shot at their wagon, and a wheel popped off. Without thinking, Emmet plucked it out of the air just as the wagon spun out of control toward a canyon cliff. Wyldstyle tugged at the reins to try to gain control, but it was no use.

"Oh, no!" Vitruvius screamed. "The wheel!"

"I can't control it much longer!" Wyldstyle tried to steer, but the pig wagon was careening wildly toward the cliff's edge.

"Emmet," Vitruvius said calmly, "we need to attach the wheel to something that spins around."

"Okay, then," Emmet said, turning his head to look for something. Suddenly, he had a stroke of inspiration. He popped off his hair and stuck the wheel to his head. Then he stepped on the peg where the axle used to be, using his body as the wagon's axle!

With the wheel back in place and Emmet's head spinning like crazy, Wyldstyle regained control of the wagon just in time to prevent them from falling into the ravine. Sheriff Not-a-Robot and his men weren't so lucky. They skidded over the edge.

"Hey, I did it, huh?!" Emmet said, still spinning.

"Well done, Emmet," Vitruvius said.

"You actually did it," added Wyldstyle. She sounded a little bit impressed.

Just when they thought they'd escaped danger, they heard the sound of a train approaching. The pig wagon was traveling too fast to stop in time! They crashed into the side and flew up into the air.

"We're gonna die!" gasped Emmet.

A split second later, they landed on the train's roof.

"*Whew!* That was close." Wyldstyle panted. "*Uh-oh . . .*"

Behind them, Bad Cop's car surged forward

and somehow managed to drive onto the top of the train car behind them.

"Get off my train," Bad Cop growled.

"Wyldstyle?" Emmet cried.

"Rest in pieces!" Bad Cop said, aiming a blaster at them.

Emmet dove, pushing Wyldstyle out of Bad Cop's way. *"Oww!"* he cried. He'd gotten hit on the back of the leg. But they were safe . . . for the moment.

A minute later, Bad Cop was closing in on them again. "He's going to ram us!" Vitruvius warned.

"Build a ramp!" Wyldstyle said. "Quick! Give me that piece! And that piece." She quickly assembled the pieces and turned the roof of the train into a skate ramp. Bad Cop's car slid right off it!

But that was far from the end of Bad Cop. He pulled a lever, and his car converted into a high-speed flying car. A moment later, he was behind them again.

"What the heck?" cried Wyldstyle.

Bad Cop grinned from the driver's seat of his jet-car. "*Aloha* means 'hello' *and* 'good-bye.'" He pulled the trigger and used his car's laser cannons to blow up the bridge. The train went hurtling over the edge.

Emmet, Wyldstyle, and Vitruvius plummeted toward the bottom of the canyon below.

"Hey," Wyldstyle called to Emmet. "Thanks for saving my life back there. Even if, you know, eventually it turned out to be pointless."

"Well, for what it's worth, this has been the greatest fifteen minutes of my life," Emmet shouted back.

As they hurtled toward a river filled with snapping cop-crocs, Emmet and Wyldstyle smiled at each other. They'd started this thing together, and they were going to end it together. . . .

But wait!

In the final seconds before they crashed into the waiting crocodile jaws, Emmet, Vitruvius, and Wyldstyle were swept to safety . . . by *Batman*!

"What the—?" Bad Cop spluttered.

"Relax, everybody," Batman said confidently. "I'm here."

"Whoa!" Emmet said, admiring his Batwing plane.

"Batman!" Wyldstyle squealed.

"What's up, babe?" said Batman. "I was totally going to call you earlier, but then I didn't."

"Babe?" Emmet asked.

"Oh, sorry," Wyldstyle explained. "Batman, this is Emmet. Emmet, this is my boyfriend, Batman."

"I'm Batman."

"Great. Where'd you guys meet?" Emmet asked.

"It's actually a funny story, right, ba —" Wyldstyle began. Before she could finish, Batman had launched himself onto Bad Cop's jet-car.

Batman grinned. "*Police* to meet you, Bad Cop."

"The pleasure is all *spine*," replied Bad Cop, chopping Batman on the back.

"Guess what? Your car is a baby carriage." Batman punched Bad Cop, and then reassembled his car into a baby carriage. The carriage plummeted into the river below, taking Bad Cop and Batman with it!

"Oh my gosh!" cried Emmet. "Your boyfriend's gone. . . ." Suddenly, Batman swooped up next to them. "Oh."

"Isn't he fantastic?" Wyldstyle gushed as Batman scrambled on board.

"Hey, babe."

Wyldstyle and Batman cooed over each other, making Emmet uncomfortable. "Uh, aren't we supposed to be heading to some secret realm or something?" he asked, trying to break the kissy mood.

Batman puffed out his chest. "I got this."

Batman flew the Batwing toward the sunset . . . and smashed right through it!

9

A moment later, Batman had converted the Batwing back into the Batmobile. Now they were speeding through a forest on the other side of the sun. Batman, Emmet, Wyldstyle, and Vitruvius gazed at a beautiful castle and a waterfall in the distance.

"Uh, is this Cloud Cuckoo Land?" asked Emmet. "Because I don't see any clouds or any cuckoos."

"No, this is Middle Zealand," Vitruvius said, "a wondrous land of knights, castles, mutton, diseases, repression, illiteracy, and, uh . . ."

"DRAGON!" Emmet cried as one shot past them, breathing fire. Batman dodged it artfully.

"Yeah, right, dragons," Vitruvius said. "Now, if we're going to get to Cloud Cuckoo Land, we need to—"

"Yeah, yeah, anyway," Batman interrupted. "You guys gotta check out these new subwoofers I installed in the back. I call 'em the dogs. Listen to 'em bark."

The bass thumped and pounded. Emmet cringed. "Can you turn it down a little bit?"

"What?! This is a song I wrote for Wyldstyle," Batman boasted. "'Darkness.' It's about how I'm an orphan."

Wyldstyle turned to Emmet. "This is important music. Dark. Brooding," Wyldstyle said.

"Well," Emmet grumbled, "I can be dark and brooding, too. . . ." His eyes lit up as he leaned out the window. "Hey, guys, look—a rainbow!"

"So you're gonna drive up the curved part, take it all the way to the top, and park the car," Vitruvius told Batman.

Batman did as the wizard instructed. They went up the rainbow and parked at the crest. Then they all scrambled out of the Batmobile.

"Friends, welcome to Cloud Cuckoo Land. I just need to give the secret knock." Vitruvius knocked

on the cloud once, and a door opened to a burst of upbeat music and a flash of colored lights.

Inside the cloud was the strangest place Emmet had ever seen. There were swirly buildings and plants that weren't shaped like anything Emmet had ever seen before. Weird creatures, bizarre robots, and crazy animals were dancing all around, enjoying their bizarre surroundings.

"O-*kaaay* . . ." Emmet said, taking it all in. "So *this* is Cloud Cuckoo Land. That makes sense."

"Hiiii!" An adorable unicorn-kitten hybrid bounced over to them. "I am Princess UniKitty, and I welcome you all to Cloud Cuckoo Land!"

"I'm just gonna come right out: I have no idea what's going on or what this place is. At all." Emmet's eyes were wide with amazement as he looked first at UniKitty, and then at all the other crazy characters and swirly kaleidoscopes whirling around them. "There's no signs on anything! How does anyone know what *not* to do?"

"Well, we have no rules here. There is no government, no bedtimes, no baby-sitters, no frowny faces, no bushy mustaches, and no negativity of any kind," explained UniKitty.

Wyldstyle put her hands on her hips. "You just said the word *no*, like, a thousand times."

UniKitty smiled at her sweetly. “And there’s also NO consistency.”

“I hate this place,” Batman moaned.

“So do you guys have laws here or building codes or gravity?” Emmet asked.

“Any idea is a good idea,” UniKitty continued. “Except the not-happy ones. Those you push down deep inside where you’ll never, ever, ever, EVER find them.” She began to get upset, but then just as quickly went back to her adorable self again. “Your fellow Master Builders are gathered in the Dog.”

None of this makes any sense, Emmet thought. He was totally confused. Aloud, he said, “The — what?”

“Is that the Green Ninja?” Emmet asked when they got to a dog-shaped meeting area a few minutes later. There were about fifty Master Builders gathered inside the secret meeting place.

Vitruvius strode onto center stage and addressed the group. “My fellow Master Builders, including but not limited to: Robin Hood, Mermaid Queen, Abraham Lincoln, 1980-something space guy, Wonder Woman, and Lagoon Creature.” All the popular Minifigures nodded when he called their names. “You have traveled far to be here for

a moment of great import. We have learned that Lord Business plans to unleash a fully weaponized Kragle on Taco Tuesday, to end the world as we know it."

All the Master Builders chattered nervously, discussing the situation.

"Please calm yourselves, Superman, Dracula, Green Ninja, Michelangelo, Johnny Thunder, and Cleopatra. There is yet one hope." Vitruvius raised his hand in the air. "The Special has arisen."

Emmet waved feebly.

"Have the young man step forward," a voice called from the crowd.

Vitruvius nodded. "As you wish. Here we go!" He gestured for Emmet to come out. "Come on, now."

"M'kay," Emmet mumbled. "Hello. I'm Emmet. Oh, and this is the Piece of Resistance." He turned around and revealed the Piece, which was still stuck to his back.

All the Master Builders *ooh*ed and *aah*ed.

"'Ooray for ze Special!" the Statue of Liberty cheered.

Emmet smiled. "Thank you. Well, I know that I, for one, am very excited to work with you guys to get into the Octan Tower and find the Kragle and put this thing on the thing. And I know it's going to be really hard, but—"

A boom of cannon fire cut him off. "Really hard?" a raspy voice demanded.

A huge, looming figure stepped forward, and Emmet gasped. The voice belonged to a gigantically tall pirate who was built entirely out of cool-looking pirate-ship parts, with a regular yellow Minifigure head on top. "Blowing your nose with a hook for a hand is 'really hard.' And not entirely effective. This be impossible. Me crew and me once stormed Lord Business's office. The result was a massacre too terrible to speak of."

"Who are you?" Emmet asked, looking up at him nervously.

"It's all right, Metal Beard," Vitruvius said. "We've all heard the—"

"But I shall speak of it all the same!" Metal Beard boomed. "We arrived at the foot of the tower only to find the Kragle was all the way up on the infinitieth floor, guarded by a robot army and security measures of every kind imaginable. Lasers. Sharks. Overbearing assistants. Strange, dangerous relics that entrap, snap, and zap . . ."

The Master Builders started murmuring among themselves.

"We faced them bravely. But our limbs were strewn everywhere!" Metal Beard continued.

Emmet was getting really uncomfortable with this story. "All right—"

The pirate would not be silenced. "I barely made it out with just me head and me organs. I had to replace every part of my once strapping, virile pirate body with this useless hunk of garbage ye see before ye. *Arrr*, it makes me furious!"

Metal Beard turned and looked Emmet straight in the eye. "So if ye think it be a good idea to return to that godforsaken place, Special, what idea have ye that's different from the ideas of a hundred of yer fallen Master Builder brothers?"

"Well . . . well, technically, I'm not, uh, not exactly a Master Builder yet," Emmet stuttered.

Everyone gasped. There was a moment of silence as everyone stared at Emmet in shock.

"What?" growled Metal Beard.

"Yes, it's true," Emmet said, trying to calm everyone down. "I may not be a Master Builder. I may not have a lot of experience fighting, or leading, or coming up with plans, or having ideas in general. In fact, I'm not all that smart. And I'm not what you'd call a creative type. Plus, I'm generally unskilled." Emmet paused for a moment, hoping to bring his speech to an inspirational conclusion. "I know what you're thinking: He's

the least qualified person in the world to lead us. And you are right."

Everyone booed. The Lagoon Creature cried out, "This is supposed to make us feel better?"

"No, no," Emmet said. "I was about to say *but*—"

"Ye all be on yer own," Metal Beard said. He stormed out of the Dog and onto his ship, where he pulled up anchor. The ship dropped out of the clouds into the sea and sailed away.

The other Master Builders looked at one another in shock. Then they got up as one and started to follow Metal Beard's lead. As they passed Emmet, they heckled and hissed at him.

"Hey, come on, guys—" Emmet pleaded. "Why are you leaving?"

Abraham Lincoln *tsk-tsked*. "A house divided against itself would be better than this!" He pressed a button on his chair, and it instantly lifted into the air and flew away.

"No, don't go, Abraham Lincoln!" Emmet called after him.

The remaining Master Builders booed and jeered, shouting, "Shame!"

"Hey, come on—we can still do this!" Emmet cried. He felt awful. This wasn't how he'd intended for things to go at all.

"You're right, he is a ding-dong," Batman whispered to Wyldstyle. "Nice one, Brickowski."

Emmet's shoulders slumped. "Well, at least it can't get any worse."

As soon as he finished speaking, Emmet realized just how wrong he was. A golf ball — which looked like a giant, earth-shattering asteroid to the LEGO figures — flew at them from above. It bounced through their meeting place, shattering it to pieces.

"I was wrong!" Emmet screamed.

10

A battalion of police planes zoomed through a hole in the clouds. Robot SWAT figures and Skeletrons rappelled down onto the surface of the cloud.

Bad Cop directed the attack from his hovering jet-car. “Ruh-roh, it’s the bad guys!” he declared gleefully. “Take all the Master Builders prisoner!”

“How did he find us?” Emmet asked.

“Go! Run!” cried Wyldstyle. “Come on, everyone, protect the Special!”

The Mermaid Queen pointed to Emmet. “What’s that on his ankle?” she asked in alarm.

Everyone looked at Emmet's ankle, where a blinking brick lit up like a homing beacon.

"It's a tracking device!" Michelangelo gasped. "He's led them right to us."

"Guys!" Emmet choked out. "No no no, it's not my fault. . . ."

The golf ball slammed down again, smashing what little remained into pieces.

"Ugh," Batman grumbled. "You are the worst leader I've ever seen. To the Batmobile!"

As he rushed to his snazzy car, a flying police ship shot a laser at it and blew it to smithereens.

"Dang it! Every man for himself. Let's go!" Batman shouted.

"No, we must protect the Piece!" Superman cried. He threw a car at one of the police ships, but the car split into pieces as soon as it hit. "It didn't break!"

"Because it's Kragled, Master Builder!" Bad Cop screamed back. "Fire machine gum!" He launched a gum-chewing device, which spit a gross wad of gum at Superman, leaving him stuck and useless. "Now, where is that Special?"

A drop ship landed and deployed a jillion robot soldiers — all hunting for Emmet.

"Babe!" Wyldstyle called to Batman. "Help me get him out of here."

"Batman works alone!" Batman shouted.

"Babe, we talked about this. You gotta be there for me."

"Fine. Fine. Fine fine fine fine *fine*." Batman sighed. "Fine!"

"And I need you to have a better attitude about it."

"I have a great attitude!" Batman knocked out a few robots. Then he pulled the tracking device off Emmet's leg, attached it to a Batarang, and flung it away.

Bad Cop was following the tracking device's signal. "The Special's in the northwest quadrant. We've got him cornered. Wait, where'd he go?"

"Ninjago!" the Green Ninja cried. He was using Spinjitzu to fight off a dozen robots. Until . . . a human-sized plastic cup fell over him, trapping him. "Really spun myself into that one." He sighed.

Wyldstyle beckoned to Batman. "Come on!" she yelled as they rushed toward an emergency exit at the edge of the cloud.

"Can't we build something to fly out of here?" Emmet asked.

As they considered his idea, a spaceman ran up and said, "Hey, I'm Ben. Ben Spaceman. But you can call me Benny! And I can build a spaceship! Watch this." He chanted, "Spaceship! Spaceship! Spaceship!" as he threw bricks together and

started to create a classic 1980-something-style LEGO spaceship.

Wyldstyle looked up and realized that they were surrounded by airships. "Okay, no. We're surrounded. The skies are filled up. There's nowhere we can go where they won't find us."

Benny's shoulders slumped. "Yeah, that's okay. I didn't really wanna build a spaceship anyway. That's cool." He kicked the half-built spaceship away in disappointment.

"Where can we go where we can't be found?" UniKitty squeaked as she bounded over to them.

Emmet peered into the ocean below. "Well, maybe we could go underwater . . . ?"

"Hey, what if we went underwater?" Batman blurted.

"Great idea, babe," Wyldstyle said.

"Thank you, Batman," UniKitty purred. "Your ideas are the best."

"But, hey," Emmet whined. "I just said that—"

"We could build a submarine," Wyldstyle said, interrupting him.

"A Bat-Submarine. Patent pending," Batman put in.

"Like an underwater spaceship!" Benny cheered.

"With rainbows!" UniKitty giggled.

"And dream catchers, in case we take a nap," Vitruvius cut in.

"Well, you can't build them all at once," Emmet reminded them.

Everyone ignored him. "Ready . . . break!"

Emmet watched uselessly as the others scattered to find pieces for their getaway vehicle.

"Here's the pieces," said Wyldstyle. "Let's put them in a big pile right here."

"Those are mine," Batman said, pointing at a few pieces the others were using.

"I'm thinking aerodynamic, but with a big personality . . . more graffiti!" Wyldstyle went on.

"Graffiti? Are you kidding? It needs to be a bat."

"Uh, you only have one idea. Bats," Wyldstyle said, shaking her head.

"You just said 'bats.' That's all I heard."

"Okay, I think we could put a wing here . . . and a rocket here . . ." said Benny.

"Ew!" Wyldstyle said, shoving Benny aside. "Get your space stuff out of my area."

"Hey, guys, can I help?" Emmet asked.

UniKitty dragged a bunch of pieces to her building area. "These are the colors I need: mountain cherry, extreme watermelon, and sour apple."

"I only work in black. And sometimes very, very dark gray," Batman explained.

"Could I just have this one tiny black brick?" Wyldstyle asked.

"You know what? I need that," Batman told her.

"All right, guys, just tell me exactly what to do," Emmet said. "And how to do it."

"Emmet, you don't need anyone to tell you what to do," Vitruvius advised. "Just do your own thing, man."

Suddenly, the ground they were standing on lurched to one side. The whole world tilted, and the half-built submarine slid away from them.

"Oh, no!" UniKitty whimpered. "They've hit our silly cloud stabilizers!"

"Go, go! We've got to finish it on the move!" cried Wyldstyle, running after their escape vehicle.

Inside the submarine, Emmet looked around and began building. He was determined to contribute, no matter what. Slowly, he clicked pieces together in a very organized way as the others argued around him.

The world continued to tilt, and the submarine slipped and slid as they scurried to finish it. Pieces tumbled around them as they fled from Bad Cop's ships and robots, all of which were firing at them from above.

As the submarine lurched to the other side and slid past their pursuers, Bad Cop cried out, "There

he is! All units attack whatever the heck that thing is! Stop him. Stop him! Don't let him get to the water."

Emmet and the others kept building, stacking bricks to create something that only vaguely resembled a submarine. Their getaway vehicle kept changing as people switched up other people's designs.

Bad Cop zoomed toward them while Batman hustled to finish the propeller, which was sleek, black, and bat-shaped. Vitruvius rushed to complete the hull, and Wyldstyle scrambled to get the conning tower put together. Everyone was building in their own way, so the submarine barely fit together.

"Quick!" UniKitty called as Bad Cop bore down on them with his missiles. "Everybody inside!"

As soon as they were inside the submarine, the ground pitched so it was completely vertical. The sub slid off the edge of the clouds and plummeted toward the ocean below.

Splash! The sub dove into the water, leaving all of the flying cop cars in its wake.

"Darn!" shouted Bad Cop, throwing his chair out the window of his jet-car.

Down, down, down Emmet and the Master Builders dove in the rickety mess of a submarine.

"My home . . . it's gone!" UniKitty whispered. "I feel something inside. It's like—the opposite of happiness. I must . . . stay . . . positive. . . . BUBBLE GUM! Butterflies!" She choked back a sob. "Cotton candy?"

"Gosh, I'm sorry, UniKitty. Do you want to talk about it?" Emmet felt awful and guilty. He gestured to a couch behind him, offering UniKitty a seat.

"What the heck is that?" Batman asked, pointing at the couch.

"Oh. It's a double-decker couch, which seemed like a good idea at the time, but I now realize is not super helpful. But it does have cup holders, and the seats flip up with coolers underneath!"

Batman shook his head. "You are so disappointing on so many levels."

"Why are my pants cold and wet?" Vitruvius said suddenly.

They all looked down—the floor was underwater!

"The walls are crying!" UniKitty squealed as more water and bricks leaked from the walls.

"We're coming apart at the seams!" Benny screeched.

With a *crrrrrack,* the submarine broke into pieces, and everyone was tossed into the sea.

Searchlights cut the water as Bad Cop and his team inspected the floating debris. "Micromanagers, is that the wreckage of a submarine?"

"Yes," the micromanagers said. "Scanning above water . . . no sighting. Scanning below water . . . no sighting. Scanning submarine wreckage . . . no life-forms detected."

"Master Builders. I knew they couldn't work together. Too many egos!" Bad Cop said, shaking his head.

"Scuba cops, recover the bodies. Dredge the entire ocean if you have to. We have to find that Piece or Lord Business is gonna lose his bananas."

11

Back in Lord Business's office tower, Bad Cop supervised as his team marched the group of captured Master Builders toward their new master.

"Hello, everybody! Nice to see you guys! Welcome to my Think Tank!" said Lord Business as he pushed a button. The ceiling peeled back. Above them, thousands of other Master Builders were strapped into machines.

"All the Master Builders you've captured over the years . . ." Superman cried. "You're using *us* against *us*?!"

"You're a very perceptive person, Superman," said Lord Business. "They come up with the instructions for everything in the universe. But the Think Tank doesn't ask politely for the instructions. It takes them against your will. ROBOTS! Seal him with the Tees of Garbaj-ay."

"No!!!" shrieked Superman.

Bad Cop and his men began to put the Master Builders into brain-sucking cells.

Lord Business scanned the faces of the gathered Master Builders. Someone was definitely missing. "Um, Bad Cop, is this all the Master Builders?"

"Yes, all the survivors, sir," Bad Cop replied. "The Special and the Piece of Resistance are at the bottom of the ocean. My scuba team is looking for his remains as we speak."

"But you don't have him? He could still be alive! The Piece could still be out there! Come on, man!" Lord Business groaned.

"Sir, I promise you, you have nothing to worry about," Bad Cop said. "We did a thorough ocean scan, and the only remnants of the Special are a double-decker couch."

"Wait. Hold on. A double-decker couch?" Lord Business said.

Bad Cop nodded. "It was floating in the ocean."

"Really? That is the most useless idea I've ever heard," Lord Business said. "If you're sitting on the bottom, and you're watching TV, are you going to have to watch through a bunch of dangling legs? Who is going to want to sit on the bottom?"

 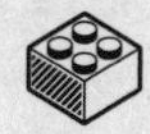 

At that moment, out on the ocean, the couch cushions on Emmet's double-decker couch flipped up, and he, Batman, Wyldstyle, Benny, UniKitty, and Vitruvius climbed out of the coolers. They clambered onto the couch as it bobbed across the water.

"The double-decker couch," Wyldstyle mused. "I guess it wasn't totally pointless."

"It's the one thing that stayed together," Benny agreed.

Vitruvius smiled. "I always believed in you, Emmet."

"One, two, three . . ." Benny said.

"Hooray for Emmet!" Wyldstyle, Vitruvius, UniKitty, and Benny cheered together.

"You know, I don't mean to spoil the party, but does anyone else notice we're stuck in the middle of the ocean on this couch?" Batman fumed. "I mean, it's not like a great big gigantic ship is going

to come out of nowhere and rescue us—"

Batman's tirade was interrupted by the sound of cannon fire. *BLAM!*

It was Metal Beard and his awesome pirate ship, the *Sea Cow*. "Avast, mateys! I have returned!" Metal Beard leaned over the ship's rails and hauled Emmet, Wyldstyle, Batman, Benny, Vitruvius, and UniKitty onboard.

"Metal Beard? Didn't you say we were a lost cause?" said Emmet.

"Ye are," Metal Beard said agreeably. "Did ye not hear me whole story circumscribing the folly of this enterprise?"

"It's kind of hard not to hear when you're shouting everything," said Batman.

"So why did you come back?" asked UniKitty.

"This bedoubled land-couch," Metal Beard explained. "Something no one ever dared to think of before. I watched Lord Business's forces overlook it completely. Which means we need more ideas like it."

Emmet smiled. "Oh, thank you!"

"Ideas so dumb and bad that no one would ever think they could possibly be useful," Metal Beard continued.

"Oh. Thank you," said Emmet, visibly deflated.

"So, Special, what do we do?" Vitruvius asked.

"Well," said Emmet. "What is the last thing Lord Business expects Master Builders to do?"

"Build a spaceship?" Benny suggested.

"Kill a chicken?" said Vitruvius.

"Marry a marshmallow?" UniKitty piped up.

"Why, this!" Metal Beard burst into a random song-and-dance routine.

"No." Emmet held up his hand. "Follow the instructions."

Everyone groaned. Batman's groan lasted way longer than anyone else's. Way, *way* longer.

"Babe," Wyldstyle said at last.

". . . aaagghhhhhhhhhh," Batman went on. "Okay, I'm done."

"Wait, guys, listen," Emmet said slowly. "You're all so imaginative and talented. You can build stuff out of thin air. But you can't work together as a team. And that's why you fell apart at the seams. I'm just a construction worker. But when I had a plan and we were all working together, we could build a skyscraper. Now, you're all Master Builders. Just imagine what could happen if you work together. You could save the universe! And that, my friends, is lesson three."

There was a moment of silence as everyone absorbed this.

Vitruvius spoke first. "Well said, Emmet. Well said."

“Really?” Emmet asked.

“She be a fine speech,” Metal Beard said.

“All right!” Emmet said. “Somebody get me some markers, construction paper, and glitter glue!”

12

Half an hour later, Emmet and his crew assembled in the pirate ship's war room.

"In order for us to get into the Kraglizer on the infinitieth floor of the Octan Tower, we're going to need to follow these instructions," Emmet began. He showed everyone the set of hand-drawn instructions he'd made up. "I call this 'Emmet's Plan to Get Inside the Tower, Put the Piece of Resistance on the Kragle, and Save the World.' I've built a hundred buildings just like this back in Bricksburg. If we can just get in there, I know where all the wiring and air ducts are located. I can get us anywhere."

"But how will we get inside?" Vitruvius asked.

"The entrance be all the way up in outer space!" Metal Beard protested.

"In a spaceship," Emmet explained.

Benny jumped up and down. "Spaceship!"

"Great idea," Batman said. "A Bat-Spaceship!"

"No. They're expecting us to show up in a Bat-Spaceship. Or a pirate spaceship. Or a rainbow-sparkle spaceship . . ."

"One of those sounds awesome to me," said Batman.

"My idea is to build a ship that's exactly like all the other Octan delivery spaceships," Emmet went on.

Benny glanced over. He'd already started to build a classic spaceship. "So, not the special spaceship that I'm building for all of you right now?"

"Sorry, Benny. Maybe next time."

Benny sighed. "You're really letting the oxygen out of my tank here."

They got to work building a delivery ship according to Emmet's instructions. "All right. Step one: Build the ship. We need a red four-piece unit over at the—UniKitty! You're supposed to follow the instructions, remember?"

UniKitty looked up sheepishly. She'd gathered a pile of sparkly bricks and used them to create flowers to decorate the wings. "Sorry."

Wyldstyle reached forward to put a piece exactly where it was supposed to go. "Oh, this gives me the jeebies."

Soon they'd finished, and the delivery ship looked perfect—exactly like the one in the instruction booklet.

"Nice!" Emmet said admiringly. "Now, step two: We pilot the ship to the service entrance of the Tower."

They zoomed toward the Tower, joining a line of other ships that looked identical to Emmet's ship.

They slipped through the gates and headed for the security check, where a robot guard stopped them. "Space ID?"

"I have a drive-on," Batman announced from his seat at the controls.

"Who are you here to see?" the guard demanded.

"I'm here to see your tush!" Batman growled.

"Is that last name Tush, first name Tush, or is it—oh my gosh!" Just as the robot realized something was amiss, Batman knocked him out with a Batarang.

"Okay, step three: We break into Lord Business's office," said Emmet. "We'll plunder his

collection of relics for disguises. Then step four: Benny and Metal Beard will sneak their way into the master control room. Once inside, they'll use their technical know-how to disable the Kragle shield."

As they sneaked through the corridors, Metal Beard and Benny heard robot guards approaching. They jumped back against a wall and quickly disguised themselves as a photocopier and a trash can.

The robots looked at each other when they spotted the photocopier. "Are you thinking what I'm thinking?" one asked.

"Do it!" said the other. The first guard climbed on top of the photocopier and started Xeroxing his tush.

Metal Beard immediately un-transformed and blasted the guards with his cannon.

Benny popped out of his trash can costume. "Metal Beard, that was awesome!"

"Fourth law of the sea: Never place your rear end on a pirate's face," Metal Beard said grimly.

They scuttled into the control room, and Benny rushed to the command board. He stared at it, totally bewildered.

"Hello, I am the computer."

"Cool!" Benny yelped. "A talking computer! Please disable the alarm and shield systems."

"Of course . . ." said the computer. "There are no movies in your area with that title."

Benny slammed his head on the console in frustration.

Meanwhile, Vitruvius was preparing to do his part in the Think Tank . . . sort of. Step five of Emmet's plan was for the wizard to sneak into the holding area and free the Master Builders. This step relied heavily on Vitruvius's natural agility and unparalleled stealth. But when Vitruvius crept across the ledge above all the trapped Master Builders, he fell.

Oops.

Back on the ship, Emmet continued to dish out instructions. "Step six: Batman, as Bruce Wayne—"

"Bruce Wayne?" Batman interrupted. "Uh, who's that? Sounds like a cool guy."

Emmet just looked at him. "As I was saying, Bruce Wayne and UniKitty go into the boardroom to make one last change to Lord Business's plan, so that Wyldstyle and I can sneak onto the robot construction team and get past the heavily guarded Kraglizer entrance—"

"Whoa, whoa," Batman interrupted. "Go back a step. I think I should go with Wyldstyle, while you stay back here and knit a sweater."

Emmet shook his head. "I'm the one with the

Piece of Resistance, so I have to go to the Kraglizer. The instructions say *you* go to the boardroom."

Batman sighed, but he and UniKitty donned their disguises. Batman put on his Bruce Wayne business suit, while UniKitty drew her costume on with a Sharpie. A moment later, she was decked out in fake eyeglasses and a tie and collar.

Inside the boardroom, Lord Business boomed, "I move that we freeze the universe. Can I get a second on that?"

Batman marched in, ready to play along. "I second. Bruce Wayne here, CEO of Wayne Enterprises. We'd like to invest in your company. Your weapon to control the universe sounds super sweet, I must say."

Lord Business patted himself on the back. "It is, indeed, super sweet."

"Cool. What kind of sound system does it have?"

"Uh . . . sound system? Well, I mean . . . we have an iPod shuffle."

Bruce Wayne shook his head. "Wait a second, you're telling me that you have a machine to control the universe and you can't listen to tunes in surround sound?"

UniKitty rolled her eyes. "Embarrassing."

"Well, we . . ." Lord Business stammered. "Uh, well . . . we need to get that done."

One of Lord Business's robots hustled to the Think Tank, where Vitruvius was hiding among the trapped Master Builders. "We need some new instructions to build a five-hundred-watt subwoofer for the Kraglizer."

The Master Builders groaned.

"Hey, don't shoot the messenger," the robot replied.

The Master Builders all thought about the request, and soon a plan had been zapped together from their brainpower. A set of instructions was sent over to the construction floor. The construction robots filed into their spots and prepared to make the new subwoofer.

An hour earlier, back on the ship, Emmet had shared the final step of his plan. "Once the instructions are printed, Wyldstyle and I will enter the Kragle room, place the thing on the other thing, and save the universe."

Emmet looked at the instructions one last time, and that's when he noticed something strange. "Whoa, hey, I didn't draw *that* in the instructions! Is that a picture of me exploding?"

Vitruvius stroked his beard nervously. "Ah,

I didn't mention that earlier? That when you reunite the Piece with the Kragle, it might explode?"

"No," Emmet said. "But it might not, right?"

Vitruvius nodded. "Sure, sure, sure. Let's go with that."

Now that they had access to the Kragle room, Emmet was ready . . . or as ready as a Minifigure can be when he's about to activate his own possible destruction. He and Wyldstyle had covered themselves in silver foil chewing-gum wrappers from Lord Business's relic room. Now they looked like construction robots.

Emmet and Wyldstyle marched into the Kragle room carrying a large speaker. Emmet was so busy eyeing the Kragle, he accidentally backed into a real robot. *"Ow!"* he choked out.

"Quiet!" Wyldstyle shushed him.

"Who are you two?" a robot construction worker demanded.

"We are transfers from downstairs," Wyldstyle replied in a mechanical robot voice.

"Your robot voice sounds an awful lot like a human voice," Emmet whispered to her.

"Give me a break, I've never been a robot before," Wyldstyle retorted.

Emmet's eyes widened. "What do you mean? You have always been a robot." He glanced at the

other robot workers, who were now surrounding them. "No no no, do not listen to her."

"What are your serial numbers?" one of the robots asked.

Suddenly, the robots' eyes began to glow red.

Panicked, Emmet began to sing in a robot voice, *"Everything is awesome . . ."*

"No way. This is my jam," a robot announced.

"This is also my jam," another robot agreed.

Emmet began to sing along with all the other robots. *"Everything is awesome . . . Everything's cool, yeah, and everything's clean . . ."* He glared at Wyldstyle, who was the only one who didn't fit in. She was going to be destroyed if she didn't play along!

"I don't want to sing the song. I'm not . . ." Wyldstyle hissed. Then she looked at the rest of the robots, and at Emmet, and suddenly she began to sing quietly.

Everything is awesome!
Everything is cool when you're part of a team.
Everything is awesome!
We're living our dream.

By the end of the song, Wyldstyle was totally into it. She pulled the robots into a conga line and they danced around the room.

". . . Fitting in is our dreeeeeeeam!" She cut off, and then whispered, "Quick, let's go!"

Emmet and Wyldstyle raced toward the Kragle while the robots were distracted. They found a grate in the wall and slipped into a crawl space. They shinnied past tubes and gears, making their way up through the wall toward the Kragle.

"I thought you didn't like that song," Emmet whispered.

"I don't."

"Mm-hmm," said Emmet skeptically. "You know, you put on this tough act, but I don't think you're as mean as you're trying to seem."

"Mean?" Wyldstyle hissed. "I'm not mean! What are you talking about?"

"I'm just saying, you were all, 'He's not the Special, Vitruvius. He can't possibly be the Special. This guy? Are you kidding me?'" Emmet reminded her. "Anyway, I don't think that's you. The real you, anyway."

Wyldstyle blushed. "Look, Emmet. I wanted it to be me, okay? I wanted to be the Special. And I know that sounds super mature, it's just—ever since I heard the prophecy, I wanted to be the one. I was right there in that construction site, right on top of it. And then it turned out to be you."

She and Emmet stopped in front of a grate. The Kragle was right across from them on a platform

in the middle of the room. Robots surrounded it.

Emmet gulped. "That night in the city, when you thought I was the Special, and you said I was talented and important? That was the first time anyone had ever really told me that. And it made me want to do everything I could to be the guy you were talking about."

Wyldstyle smiled. "Lucy."

"What?"

"That was my real name. You asked earlier, and it's Lucy."

"I really like that name."

They reached for each other, but then Batman popped out of one of the ceiling tiles. "Hey, what are you two losers talking about?"

"*Huh,* what?" Wyldstyle said nervously. "I just . . . What?"

"Thought I'd help you guys out here. Left the weird cat-thing to stall back in the boardroom," said Batman.

Back in the boardroom, UniKitty was busy bamboozling the robots with her business jargon. She was very convincing. "Business business business. Numbers. Is this working?"

"Yes," answered one of the robots. He looked impressed.

Emmet and Wyldstyle were waiting behind the grate leading to the Kragle room. Emmet broke

away from Wyldstyle. "There's Bad Cop right there," he said, pointing to the surveillance room opposite them.

Wyldstyle smiled at him. "Good luck, Emmet."

"Lucy! I guess this might be good-bye."

She waved her hand in the air, dismissing him. "I don't like good-bye, so let's just call this, 'see you later, alligator.'"

Batman looked around. "Lucy? Who's Lucy?"

Emmet didn't answer. "Batman, when we get inside this room, they're gonna have audio sensors as well as motion sensors, so we have to be really quiet."

"Yeah, yeah, I read your dumb instructions."

Emmet held his communicator to his mouth. "Benny! What's our status with the shield?"

Benny sounded totally panicked. "Uh . . . we're trying to deactivate the shield. It's just a little frustrating. . . ."

As he spoke, Emmet could hear a computer voice saying, "Downloading latest episode of *Where Are My Pants?*"

"Where are you getting pants from?! I never said pants!" Benny screeched.

Beside the Kragle, Bad Cop's phone rang. "Bad Cop here."

It was Wyldstyle on the line! "Hi. This is Lord

Business's assistant," she said in a robot voice. "He would like you to come to his office immediately."

"Copy. Thanks."

"You are welcome, sir."

As Bad Cop headed out of the electric security doors, Wyldstyle threw her phone between the doors before they could close all the way. They were jammed open!

Wyldstyle rushed in, quickly disposing of the remaining robots. Then she waved Batman and Emmet the all clear.

"That's the signal," Emmet told Batman. "But the shield's still up."

"We'll wing it. That's a bat pun. Because bats have wings." He sighed. "It doesn't work when I have to explain it. Let's just go."

Batman threw a grappling hook toward the ceiling of the Kragle's inner sanctum. Then he swept up Emmet, and the two of them swung toward the Kragle.

Emmet put his communicator to his mouth again. "Benny, disable the shield now!"

Inside the control room, Benny was having some problems. The computer chirped, "Searching for Albanian restaurants . . ."

Benny threw his hands up in the air. "What? No! I never once said—"

The computer cut him off. "I don't understand what you mean."

"Disable . . . the . . . shield!" cried Benny.

"Benny?" Emmet whispered into the communicator as he and Batman swung to and fro. "What's going on?"

Suddenly, Emmet heard Metal Beard in the background. "Aye, Benny—I'll do it meself." He spoke directly to the computer. "Be ye disabling of yon shield," he commanded.

"Disabling shield," the computer replied.

"What?!" cried Benny. He couldn't believe it.

The laser shield protecting the Kraglizer was finally down!

"Okay, in three, two, one . . . Let's do this!" Emmet swung forward and landed on the platform right next to the Kragle. Moving carefully, he positioned himself beneath the nozzle of the glue tube and slowly slid up, trying to fit the cap in place.

As he drew closer to the Kragle, Emmet glanced up at Wyldstyle one last time . . . and saw Bad Cop standing right behind her with a team of robot cops!

"Lucy! No!"

13

Robots shot rubber bands at Wyldstyle, body-cuffing her! Bad Cop pulled an alarm, and a shield dropped down around Emmet. He was trapped, and the Kragle was lifted out of his reach. "No!" Emmet screamed.

Robots swarmed around them. They rubber-banded Batman, who was still hanging from the ceiling. "Ah, dang it."

Alarms sounded throughout the building. In the boardroom, UniKitty was surrounded. In the

control room, a net dropped down on Benny and Metal Beard.

In the Think Tank, Vitruvius was still free. "I'm sneaking around the corner," he whispered into his walkie-talkie.

Lord Business approached him. "Vitruvius."

"Lord Business."

"I see you've wandered into my Think Tank," Lord Business sneered. "And by the way, I found a few of your friends, by which I mean . . . all of them!"

Bad Cop led Emmet, Wyldstyle, and the others into the Think Tank.

"Sorry," Emmet said, shrugging at Vitruvius.

"Acceptable work, Bad Cop." Lord Business smiled.

"Thank you, sir."

"Robots!" Lord Business demanded. "Destroy this old man once and for all!"

"Did you just call me old?" Vitruvius demanded.

"Yeah. So what?" said Lord Business.

Vitruvius quickly built a walker out of LEGO pieces. "Well, junebug, I really prefer the word *experienced*." He whipped his walker into the air and took out a bunch of Bad Cop's robots.

Emmet and the others cheered as Vitruvius fought. "Yeah!"

"Ha-ha!" Vitruvius cackled. "You see, Emmet?

A corrupted spirit is no match for the purity of imaginat—"

Suddenly, Lord Business rose up behind Vitruvius and threw a penny at him, breaking his body into pieces!

"No!" Emmet screamed.

Vitruvius's head rolled over and settled at Emmet's feet. "Vitruvius!"

"My sweet Emmet," Vitruvius's head said. "Come closer, you must know something about the prophecy. . . ."

"I know," Emmet said, choking up. "I'm doing my best, but I don't, I don't—"

"The prophecy . . . I made it up."

"What?"

"I made it up." Vitruvius's head gasped. "It's not true."

"But that means I'm just . . . I'm not the Special."

"You must listen," Vitruvius said. "What I'm about to tell you will change the course of history. . . ." But before he could utter another word, Vitruvius passed away.

Emmet cried out in despair as Vitruvius's blank eyes turned to *X*s. *"Nooooo . . ."*

Lord Business looked smug. "Not so special anymore, huh? No one ever told me *I* was special and look how I turned out—I'm awesome! I never got a trophy just for showing up. I'm not some

special little snowflake, but as unspecial as I am? *You* are a thousand, billion times more unspecial than me."

Listening to Lord Business, Emmet grew more and more glum. He'd failed! His friend and mentor was dead. And he wasn't the Special after all.

"Robots, bring me the Sword of Exact Zero," declared Lord Business gleefully.

A micromanager strapped Emmet onto a human-sized zapping battery as the rest of the gang were forced into the Think Tank's brain-sucking cells.

Lord Business continued to speak as the others worked. "Must be weird. One minute, you're the most special person in the universe, and the next minute, you're nobody." He reached forward and sliced the Piece of Resistance off Emmet's back with an X-Acto blade. "You know, I have a nice spot for this in my relic room. *Uh-oh!* My mistake!" He tossed the Piece into the infinite chasm outside his office window. "There it goes. Bye-bye forever!"

The Master Builders gasped.

"No!" Wyldstyle screamed.

"Bad Cop, you do the honors," Lord Business commanded.

"With pleasure," said Bad Cop. "Uh, release the Kragle!"

"That was the most unconvincing piece of

garbage I've ever heard," Lord Business said, shaking his head.

Bad Cop took a deep breath and tried again. "Release the Kragle?!"

"Never mind, I'll do it," said Lord Business. "Release the Kragle!" he boomed. He turned back to Bad Cop. "See, that's how it's done, son. Computer, set the timer to one hundred Mississippis. And once I've safely left the building, terminate everyone. Emmet, you'll get a front-row seat bound to this electrified monolith."

The ceiling opened. A long black tentacle reached down into the room, and Lord Business hopped onto it. "Bad Cop, unfortunately I'm going to have to leave you here to die." He waved good-bye as the tentacle lifted him out of the room.

Bad Cop looked around wildly. "What?! Sir!"

"I know," said Lord Business regretfully. "It's not personal, it's business. Lord Business. *Ciao!*"

Lord Business cranked up the power on his electric shocker, setting the timer for ten minutes. There was a loud CRACK as the entire top of the office tower broke off and floated away, taking Lord Business with it.

The countdown to total destruction was under way.

14

Outside, Lord Business's colossal Kraglizer cube flew over the ocean until it reached Bricksburg. It hovered menacingly over the city as Lord Business addressed the citizens.

"Attention, everyone. This is President Business. Hello! Hi! Welcome to Taco Tuesday. Don't worry about this big black thing that's blocking out the sun. That's not what you need to worry about. What you need to worry about is this question that I'm about to ask you: WHO WANTS A TACO?"

The crowd of Bricksburg residents cheered from below. "Tacos! Tacos!"

"Yaaay!" Lord Business shouted. "I know, I'm excited, too. All right, everyone, step one: Pretend I'm not even here. Step two: Don't panic. Step three: I want everybody to say 'Freeze!'"

Massive tentacles emerged from the bottom of Lord Business's Kraglizer and sprayed a cloudy mist on the city below. The gluey spray froze people, cars, everything.

Terrified, the Minifigures of Bricksburg scattered and ran for safety.

"So I guess running around and screaming is normal? Just listen to me!" Lord Business snapped. "Micromanagers! Commence micromanagement!"

A squad of mechanical micromanagers zoomed out of the cube's base. They swarmed the area, stopping the townspeople and posing them.

"Commencing micromanagement!" the micromanagers droned. As soon as a scene was arranged perfectly, the tentacles sprayed Kragle mist over it, freezing it into place.

The whole world was being glued into place, and the Piece of Resistance was gone for good.

They were doomed.

Back in the Think Tank, Emmet and the others watched Lord Business's path of destruction on a monitor. It was all over. They had failed.

"Emmet, what do we do?" Benny whimpered.

"Didn't you hear him?" Emmet said sadly. "The prophecy's made up. I'm not the Special. And to think for a moment I thought I might be—"

A ghostly voice cut through the gloom. "Emmet . . ."

"What? Who said that?"

"I did." Emmet turned. "I am Ghost Vitruvius," a ghost said. It was dressed in a sparkling cape and an elastic headband. "No one can see or hear me but you."

"Actually," Wyldstyle cut in, "I can hear you, and see you. You're right there."

"I can see you, too!" UniKitty said.

"Really?" Ghost Vitruvius asked. "Okay, fine. Emmet, you didn't let me finish earlier. Because I died. The *reason* I made up the prophecy was because I knew that whoever found the Piece could *become* the Special, because the only thing anyone needs to be special is to believe that you can be. I know that sounds like a cat poster, but it's true. Emmet, look at what you did when you believed you were special. You just need to believe it some more."

Emmet looked at Ghost Vitruvius pleadingly.

"But how can I just decide to believe that I'm special when I'm not?"

"You must find that answer within yourself," said Ghost Vitruvius. He smiled and floated away.

"Zapping termination in twenty Mississippis," the computer said.

Emmet looked around frantically, trying to figure out what to do. That's when he noticed there were two wires connected to the object he was bound to. This strange object—the battery—was the power source that would zap his friends and destroy them forever. He had to disconnect it!

Emmet struggled to break free from his bindings, but it was no use. Slowly, he forced his way over to the window.

The computer continued counting down. "Twenty Mississippi . . . nineteen Mississippi . . . eighteen Mississippi . . ."

"Emmet! What are you doing?" shrieked Wyldstyle. "Don't."

"Lucy, now it's your turn to be the hero," Emmet told her.

"No!!" Wyldstyle cried.

"See ya later, alligator," Emmet said, smiling at her. Then he closed his eyes, took a deep breath, and flung himself out the window after the Piece of Resistance!

15

"*Nooooo!*" cried Wyldstyle.

But it was too late. Emmet was gone.

"Five Mississippi . . . four Mississippi . . . three Mississippi . . ." said the computer. But then . . .

"Error. Termination failure," said the computer. The battery powering the termination sequence had disappeared into the abyss along with Emmet. The Think Tank shut down. Emmet had done it!

One by one, the Master Builders broke free of their bindings. Wyldstyle ran to the ledge and

stared into the infinite chasm. She could see the disconnected wires dangling, but there was no sign of Emmet.

"No . . . Emmet . . ." Wyldstyle murmured.

"What do we do now?" said UniKitty. "We have to do something!"

Superman shook his head. "We're all out of ideas. He literally took all our ideas! We might as well just watch *Where Are My Pants?*"

The other Master Builders murmured in agreement. They stared at the monitors numbly as Lord Business rampaged through Bricksburg with the Kraglizer.

"Emmet had ideas," said Benny sadly.

"*Arr.* If only there were more people in the world like he be," said Metal Beard.

"Wait a minute!" cried Wyldstyle. Metal Beard's words had given her an idea of her own. "Meet me downstairs in a sec." She dashed off.

UniKitty, Benny, and Metalbeard looked at one another in confusion. Then they followed her.

  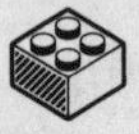

A moment later, Wyldstyle burst into the *Where Are My Pants?* TV studio.

"Honey, where are my pants?" the lead actor said. A laugh track played.

"Hey, guess what?" said Wyldstyle, handing him his pants. "I found your pants. Series is over." Then she turned to Benny, who was right behind her. "Benny, send this out to everyone in the universe."

Benny hurried over to the control room. It was filled with reel-to-reels, wires, and computer keyboards. 1980-something technology? "Now you're talking!"

The others began filming Wyldstyle as Benny broadcast the feed live to every station in the universe. "Hey, everybody, you don't know me, but I'm on TV so you can trust me."

All around Bricksburg, Minifigures turned to watch the TV screens in their living rooms and outside department stores and sports stadiums. Hundreds were watching Wyldstyle, even as Lord Business swooped overhead, Kragling people left and right.

"I know things seem really bad right now, but there is a way out of this," Wyldstyle went on. "Roll that footage, Ben."

Benny hit a button on his keyboard, and video of Emmet appeared onscreen. First there was security footage of him working at the construction site in Bricksburg, and then feed that showed him discovering the Piece of Resistance.

Wyldstyle continued speaking as the footage rolled. "This is Emmet, and he was just like all of

you—a face in the crowd, following the same instructions as you. He was so good at fitting in, no one ever saw him."

The video showed Emmet using his head as the wheel axle in the Old West and creating a double-decker couch in Cloud Cuckoo Land.

"I used to think people like Emmet were followers with no ideas or vision," Wyldstyle said. "But it turned out Emmet had great ideas, and even though they were weird and kind of pointless, they actually came closer than anything else to saving the universe. And now is the time for you to finish the job. All of you have new ideas, and if you let those ideas build off one another, we'll have an army of ideas. An army that can defeat those machines and take down that big, boring cube!"

All around Bricksburg, Middle Zealand, and the Old West, Minifigures listened to Wyldstyle.

"All of you have the ability inside of you to be a groundbreaker. And I mean literally break the ground, peel up the pieces, tear apart your walls right now," Wyldstyle finished. "Today will not be known as Taco Tuesday. It will be known as Freedom Friday. But still on a Tuesday."

"Yeah!" people cheered. "We can do it!"

At Emmet's old work site, the construction workers were moved. They began picking up pieces and putting them together.

All around Bricksburg, people were building. Inside coffee shops, on pirate ships, in the middle of the street—everyone was building.

Suddenly, robots swarmed the TV studio. "End of the line!" shouted one, aiming his blaster at Wyldstyle. But before he could shoot it, Bad Cop burst in from behind and blasted all the robots!

"Bad Cop?" said Wyldstyle, shocked.

"I hope there's still a Good Cop in me somewhere," he replied grimly. He turned his face around and drew a smiley face on the blank side. "I'll hold these guys off. You go stop 'em."

"Great idea," said Metal Beard gruffly. "But how will we get to Bricksburg?"

Benny began to hyperventilate with excitement. "I could . . . I could build a spaceship."

No one spoke for a long moment.

"You're not going to say no?!" Benny said hopefully.

Bad Cop shrugged. "Build away, whatever your name is."

Benny dropped to his knees, shedding tears of joy. He couldn't believe his ears. He shot around the room, frantically building the spaceship he had always dreamed of. "Spaceship! Spaceship! Spaceship! Spaceship!" he chanted.

Two minutes later, an awesome, slightly retro spaceship stood before him. Wyldstyle, Batman,

UniKitty, and Metal Beard scrambled on board. A moment later, they'd zoomed off, bursting through the walls dividing every realm on their quest to reach Bricksburg.

"All units attack that spaceship!" cried the robot commander. A fleet of robo-fighters charged after Benny's ship.

"Where'd he go?" demanded the robot commander.

"Spaceship! Spaceship!" cried Benny.

The ship emerged onto the streets of Bricksburg, where a wild battle was under way. The citizens of Bricksburg had converted their surroundings into an array of strange and amazing attack vehicles, and they were all aiming for Lord Business and his robots.

"Oh. My. Gosh," said Metal Beard, watching the carnage in awe.

"This is even crazier than I thought it would be!" exclaimed Wyldstyle.

"Wyldstyle, look! Cowboys!" squealed UniKitty.

"And check out those castle-ships over there," said Batman. He sounded impressed.

Larry the barista had converted his coffee shop into a flying cannon that sprayed coffee. "Mine shoots hot coffee. That'll be thirty-seven dollars!" A micromanager melted under the force of his java jets.

In the distance, the Kraglizer was spraying the city streets. Millions of micromanagers blocked our heroes' way.

Perched on top of the spaceship, Metal Beard bellowed, "Everyone, clear us a path toward that cube!"

A plumber-truck ship shot plungers at the Kraglizer's closest tentacle. The tentacle chased him around the corner, only to encounter a garbage truck that had been converted into an enormous chomper, which bit down and destroyed it.

"This might actually work," said Wyldstyle.

"'Twas your speech that roused this hearty crew," Metal Beard said.

"Thanks, guys!" cried the plumber.

Dozens of converted ships were pouring through the portal from other realms. A castle-ship, an Old West-ship, and a pirate spaceship all converged on the streets of Bricksburg.

A steady stream of Master Builders followed them. Green Lantern, the Statue of Liberty, Superman, the Lagoon Creature, and the Green Ninja all joined the fight.

"Don't forget us Master Builders!" cried Abraham Lincoln.

Inside the Kraglizer, Lord Business realized that things were not going according to plan. A converted ice-cream truck was flying around him,

playing annoying jingles and blocking his view with jets of whirling ice cream sprayed from its cone cannon. "What the H-E-C-K is going on?! This is an abomination of silliness! They aren't following my orders! Don't let them near this Kraglizer! I'm the boss! I'm the boss of you! I'm really tall!"

Back in the streets, Wyldstyle watched the fight. She couldn't believe her words had had such a powerful effect. "Benny, head for the base of that thing," she said. "You know, the Kraglizer."

Benny nodded. "Spaceship!" He expertly steered the ship toward the Kraglizer.

"We've got micromanagers swarming us," UniKitty squealed.

"Not for long," said Wyldstyle. She, Batman, Metal Beard, and UniKitty jumped onto the spaceship's wings and started beating back the micromanagers.

"*Arr*, take that, you mechanized micro-thingy!" growled Metal Beard as he blasted them with cannonballs.

"No one messes with my friend's spaceship!" cried UniKitty.

Wyldstyle turned to Batman. "Listen, Batman, we need to talk," she began. "This is hard to say, but—"

"I think we should break up," Batman interrupted. "I just wanted to say that first before

you say whatever you're going to say. I'm breaking up with you, and I said that first. And I'm Batman. First to break up. What were you going to say?"

Wyldstyle stared at him for a second. She swallowed her pride. "Nothing."

"Look, I'm sorry about Emmet," said Batman, relenting a bit. "He was a dork, but he was a good guy. If he were here, I'm sure he'd say—"

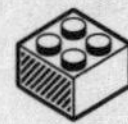 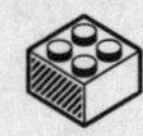 

"AAAAAAAAHHHHHHHHH!" cried Emmet as he spun in a whirling vortex of lights. He hit the ground with a crunch. Where was he?

Back in Bricksburg, things were not going well for our heroes. "Stay on course, Benny!" cried Wyldstyle.

"*Arr*, guys, I don't mean to be a stubborn barnacle, but even if we can reach that behemoth without getting Kragled, how are we going to stop it? Without that Piece, we be doomed!" Metal Beard said.

Inside the Kraglizer, Lord Business had had it. "This rebellion ends now," he declared. He watched as bevies of crazily constructed ships fought off

his micromanagers. He sent out more micromanagers, who intercepted the rebels' ships, put them back into their original shapes, and Kraglized them!

Several micromanagers overran Benny's spaceship and pulled UniKitty, Benny, Batman, and Wyldstyle off.

"We were a hearty crew, but it's . . . it's over," Metal Beard cried as he landed in a heap on top of the others.

Emmet looked around him. "Where am I?" He was in a dark, flat place, with nothing around him. Except . . . was that the Piece of Resistance? It was lying a few feet away from him. *"Whoa!"*

Emmet reached for it. "I can still save them!"

At that moment, a portal opened up in front of him. He couldn't believe it! Vitruvius's voice echoed in his head. *You need to make the final connection. . . .*

Emmet grabbed the Piece and hurtled into the portal.

16

On the streets of Bricksburg, a comet appeared in the sky. It was plummeting toward the city! It slammed into the ground, sending LEGO bricks into the air around it.

A moment later, Emmet emerged from the debris, holding the Piece of Resistance in front of him. "Sorry, street," he said.

He'd landed right near his work construction site. He looked around. Suddenly, the potential of all the LEGO pieces around him was obvious. It

was as if he was truly seeing the bricks for the first time!

"I see everything! I am a Master Builder!" Emmet exclaimed. He started quick-building himself a giant mech with caterpillar-tread feet, a steam-roller, a digger-shovel fist, and armored shoulder plates with swinging wrecking balls.

A few moments later, it was complete. Emmet jumped inside and raced toward the Kraglizer.

"Look! It's Emmet!" exclaimed Wyldstyle.

"I was the first to recognize his talent," said Metal Beard. Wyldstyle raised an eyebrow at him skeptically.

Emmet's former co-workers spotted him, too. "Hey, is that the guy we used to work with?" asked Wally.

"Yeah!" said Gail. "Eric!"

"Exactly," said Wally. "Eric."

"Lucy, I'm going inside that thing!" Emmet cried. "But I'm going to need your help."

"You got it, Emmet," Wyldstyle replied.

"Okay, here's what we're going to do. . . ."

Inside the Kraglizer's cockpit, Lord Business gnashed his teeth. "Release every micromanager we have!"

A hole opened in the bottom of the cube, and hundreds of micromanagers poured out. All

around Emmet, micromanagers were attacking. "Commencing micromanagement," they chanted.

"*Ahh* . . . no!" cried Emmet, trying to shrug them off.

UniKitty could see he was in trouble. "Emmet! No!" she wailed. She took deep breaths, trying to remain calm. "Stay positive . . . stay positive," she murmured. But she couldn't contain herself any longer.

There was an explosion of lights and flames. UniKitty transformed . . . into AngryKitty!

"*RAHHHH!* Disembowel them! You mess with the kitty, you get the horn!" She launched an all-out blitz on the micromanagers, taking out dozens of robots with a swipe of her horn and claws. "Now's your chance, Emmet! GO! GO!"

Emmet took his opportunity. He fought his way over to the cube, and then shot an enormous wrecking ball into the wall of a nearby skyscraper. Then he used it to swing up into the base of the Kraglizer.

"Sir, the gate's not closed," a robot informed Lord Business as Emmet landed right behind him. "*AAHHH!*"

Emmet tossed the robot away. "Lord Business."

"Back from the dead, Brickowski?" Lord Business sneered. "Well, you're too late! You see,

you're finished." He pulled out the Kragle and aimed it at Emmet, who managed to dodge several blasts before his leg was hit. He was glued to the floor!

"No! Stop," Emmet commanded. "If you do one more thing, I'm going to unleash my secret weapon."

"Your secret weapon?" Lord Business said scornfully.

Emmet nodded. "It's called the Power of the Special."

Lord Business rolled his eyes. "That sounds dumb."

"All right, here it comes," said Emmet. "My secret weapon is this." He extended a hand to Lord Business.

"What's that? Is it super small?" asked Lord Business. "I don't see anything."

"It's my hand," explained Emmet. "I want you to take it."

"You want me to take your hand off?"

"No, I want you to join me," Emmet replied. "You might see a mess out there—"

"Exactly," Lord Business interrupted him. "And a bunch of really weird and dorky stuff that ruined my perfectly good stuff!"

"Okay, that's what you see," said Emmet. "But what I see are people inspired by one

another—and by you. People taking what you made and making something new out of it."

Lord Business looked out the cube's windows as Emmet went on. "You are not the bad guy. You made this great big awesome amazing world. But you don't want anyone else to touch it. And that's just too bad. Because there's nothing more exciting, and fun, and scary, than making something new. And if you seal all this up forever, no one—not even you—gets to feel that feeling ever again. Instead, you just feel alone."

Lord Business's eyes filled with tears as Emmet went on.

"Someone once told me something that I'll never forget, and I'm gonna tell you right now: You are the most talented, most interesting, and most extraordinary person in the universe. And you are capable of amazing things, because you are the Special. And so am I," Emmet went on. "And so is everyone. The prophecy is made up, but it's also true. It's about all of us, and right now it's about you. And you can still change everything." He held up the Piece of Resistance.

Lord Business stared at it for a minute. Then he approached Emmet slowly . . . and hugged him!

"Oh, we've got a hugger," said Emmet.

Lord Business took the Piece of Resistance from

Emmet's hand. Then he brought it to the Kragle, put it on the nozzle, and sealed it shut!

"Be careful!" said Emmet. "I heard it might explode."

The Kragle began to quake and shake.

"Thank you, Emmet," said Lord Business. "This thing isn't going to explode, is it?"

"Sure, sure, let's go with that," Emmet replied. Just then, the Kragle exploded! A massive fireball of LEGO bricks sent Emmet flying out the window. One of his legs was stuck behind in a glob of glue. The rest of his body tumbled to the ground.

Emmet landed in a pile of rubble on the streets of Bricksburg. All around him, bricks were scattered about. In their midst were many Kragled heroes, frozen in time and place.

"Emmet!" cried Wyldstyle, Metal Beard, UniKitty, and Batman.

"Hey, everyone, are you okay?" Emmet asked.

"We did it!" cheered Wyldstyle.

Emmet reached for her hand.

Overhead, there was a sprinkle of water. It was starting to rain.

As the water fell, the glue began melting! Minifigures were breaking free from the glue and starting to move!

Overhead, Lord Business was swooping back and forth, spraying liquid from a new ship that

vaguely resembled a watering can. "*Whoops!* I have the antidote for the Kragle! How did that happen? No, really, I honestly don't know how it happened."

Back on the street, Emmet and Wyldstyle held hands. "Well, Lucy, now that we saved the universe, I can finally sit down and enjoy a meal with the special people in my life," Emmet said.

Wyldstyle smiled at him. "I guess that's what happens when we work together."

THE
MOVIE
#THELEGOMOVIE
WWW.THELEGOMOVIE.COM
VILLAGE
ROADSHOW
PICTURES
LEGO
©2013 THE LEGO GROUP
WARNER BROS. PICTURES
©2013 Warner Bros. Ent. All Rights Reserved